D1114173

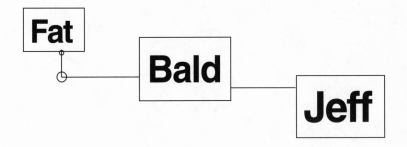

Fat Bald Jeff

a novel

Leslie Stella

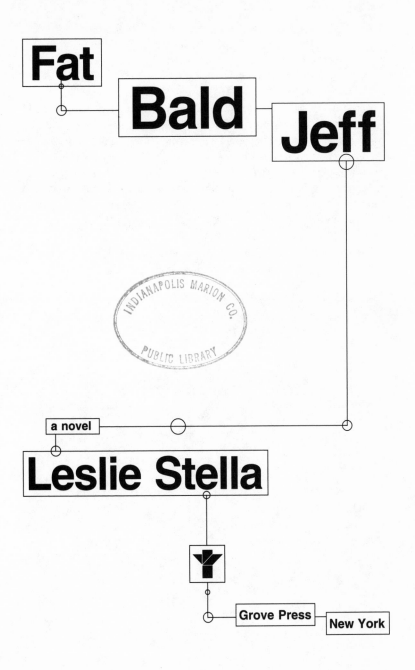

Grove Press New York

Published simultaneously in Canada
Printed in the United States of America

FIRST EDITION

Library of Congress Cataloging-in-Publication Data

Stella, Leslie.
    Fat bald Jeff : a novel / Leslie Stella.
        p. cm.
    ISBN 0-8021-3772-5
    1. Young women—Fiction.   2. Office politics—Fiction.   I. Title.
    PS3569.T37972 F37 2001
    813'.6—dc21   00-063657

Design by Laura Hammond Hough

Grove Press
841 Broadway
New York, NY 10003

To Chris

Acknowledgments

Particular thanks to my editor Amy Hundley, Amye Dyer at Lukeman Literary Management, Jim McNeill and Ben Paris for valuable advice and commentary, Jim and Nancy Stella, Lumpens everywhere, and most of all, my husband Chris, for massive amounts of love, support, and faith.

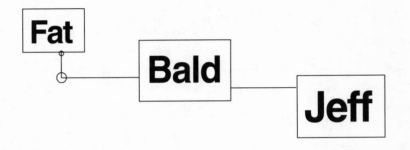

Chapter 1

Men never offer me their seats on the bus. I don't know why; nothing about me screams out self-sufficiency. As the bus chugged forward, bearing me toward another day's drudgery, I leaned against a nearby geriatric for support. The bus braked in traffic, pitching me on top of him, and the clumsy old cripple ground his umbrella tip into my instep! I elbowed him in retaliation. Late for work again. It really sticks in my craw.

I know all about punctuality. There could not be a more punctual person than I, not counting work tardiness. Even as a child I rose early every morning to awaken my drug-addled parents. They were never grateful to be shaken from their haze, but then I never expected thanks. That's just the kind of person I am.

The old man tried to trip me with his umbrella as I made my way down the bus aisle. I hit him in the head with the belt buckle of my fake Burberry, causing him to cry out. The elderly are strange, and I know we should be kind to them, given their achy, unavailing bodies and relentless grievance with humanity, but I find it difficult sometimes.

My own grandmother, though chronologically matched with the umbrella man, possesses none of the awful traits of the old. She is spry, where the average geriatric is spasmodic; she is spirited, where the other is crotchety; she is literate, where the other scans religious tracts and perhaps the Jumble.

In short, she is alive, where so many of them are simply dead boring. And she still wears chic cashmere twin sets and Cherries in the Snow lipstick, although she fools no one. She's over eighty and looks it.

The bus dumped me at my stop, and I ran the remaining four blocks to the building the National Association of Libraries calls home. As I rounded the last corner, a BMW sped by and splashed puddle water on me. A crossing slacker, no doubt on his way to a disreputable café, snickered as I tried to wring out my coat. There can be no doubt that we live in barbaric times, when pedestrians no longer assist young women splashed by passing imports. Barbaric, too, is the shoddy workmanship I've come to expect from consumer items in my price range. The knockoff Burberry's tartan lining had not been Scotchgarded at all!

Caught a glimpse of myself in the glass doors at the office entrance: knobby, pipe-cleaner legs rooted in gruel-colored galoshes, plastic rain bonnet askew yet vigilant, luminous hazel eyes, pugnacious chin. I suppose my potential has been wasted. I blame work.

Scurried in with a crowd of tardy zombies. It's sad how being an employee eventually renders one soulless. Like a mad elephant seal, the supervisor rolled into my cubicle just as I removed my moist outer garments.

Great quivering jowls, more like the earflaps of an aviator's helmet than cheeks, brushed his collar. Black-currant eyes bore down on me out of his dumpling face. He stood arms akimbo like a Sumo sugar bowl, and high-water trousers revealed an upsetting pair of ankles.

"Fifteen minutes late, Addie," he blubbered through lips as thick as a Norwegian cod's. Indeed, the lips were so massive and his rubbery cheeks so scaly and blue—and his demeanor so completely uncuddly—that they earned him the unfortunate nickname Coddles. He scolded me as I held my sopping raincoat aloft, waiting for him to finish. Finally he lumbered away, and I noted with satisfaction the trail of toilet paper stuck to the sole of his sensible shoe.

Coarse laughter sounded from beyond the cubicle walls. My office mates were sharing gossip over stale pastries, as most of the serfs around here liked to do. I picked up my coffee mug and walked back down the corridor toward the stairwell. Stinking elevator was broken again, so I had to walk down two flights of stairs to the staff cafeteria, a moldering asbestos-tiled room known as the dungeon. I had just prepared to slap my thirty-five cents down on the counter when a crude zombie pushed her way in front of me.

I said, "Pardon me" in my most severe tone, but she just turned and gave me the type of smile that frightens dogs. She stared at my mug. "Is that an armadillo?" she asked.

I suppose even zombies can appreciate quality ceramics. I firmly grasped the mug handle, or tail, and poured out my coffee, explaining how the armadillo represents the character armor I must bear against society's mediocrity. But when I looked up she was gone. Gloria, the surly Guatemalan coffee attendant, scooped my change into the cash drawer and nibbled on a dried-out bear claw.

I turned and nearly was trampled by a short yet enormous tech-support worker. He was heading for the pastry platter like a humpback whale intent on a school of plankton. It was only due to my quick reflexes, honed from years of dodging flying bits of clay from my father's lousy potting wheel, that I escaped injury. The techie grasped a fistful of crullers and shoveled them in, while I, shaken but still prepared to go on with the day, faced the two long flights back to my cubicle. Rested for a few minutes on the landing, summoning my strength for the final ascent. Why is the elevator always broken? Exercise is risky for those of us with delicate constitutions.

Imagine my chagrin when I came back down the corridor to see several zombies milling about my cubicle entrance.

"Department meeting," one said. They looked put out at having to come fetch me. I followed the rest of the publishing department—two other copyeditors, three graphic designers, some anonymous salesmen, various production slaves, the *très* hideola Coddles, and the department head, Mr. Genett—into the conference room. The zombies jockeyed for positions next to their friends. As usual, I sat by myself.

Coddles rambled for thirty minutes about the new executive bathroom, off limits to the rest of us, and the purchase of more bank art for the halls. We copyeditors had put in a request for ergonomic desk chairs, but it was denied in favor of a new microwave for the lounge and higher quality staplers. I suppose that means four more years of sitting on a folding chair in my cubicle. My office mates have already developed fleshy humps between their shoulder blades and have given up hope, though I am younger and fresher and will continue to fight. This issue is particularly dear to me since I have always prided myself on excellent posture.

Across the conference table sat my two fellow copy-editors, Bev and Lura. They occupy the cubicles on either side of me, and all day I endure their mundane inquiries about each other's pencil supply and lunch pail. Lura is all right. Her hair is unkempt, but that's what men like these days. I expect it reminds them of wild tussling in the sack. Bev, on the other hand, is a poisonous old hag and as lowbrow as Java Man. Lura gets on well with Bev, but Lura is one of those who gets along with everyone. I demand a higher standard from humankind but am usually disappointed. Consequently, I spend much time alone. I am used to it; sensitive people have always been exiled to the fringes of society. The philistines don't understand us.

Next to Bev and Lura sat the graphic designers, a triumvirate of techie duds. They wear stained pumpkin-farmer jeans and grimy grandpa sweaters, and enjoy shooting things on the computer. Then the salesmen, mostly middle-aged ghosts with brown slacks and eyes like boiled eggs. I don't have to interact with them much. The production slaves huddled together in a beleaguered pile in the corner. They are the corporate peasants of our department, trod upon and bullied by everyone else. The designers scream at them for mucking up page layout, copyeditors complain about the constant addition of new typos, and Coddles doesn't trust them with the postage meter. The production slaves are herded two to a cube in the dark, smelly wing of our department. Their nameplates are attached to the cubicle walls with Velcro.

Mr. Genett took over the podium and Coddles plumped down next to me. *Quelle* pig! I could feel his pinprick eyes on me, lingering particularly at my bust, which, though not ample by today's ridiculous standards, was at least symmetrical and secured by a too-snug dove-gray jacket I picked up at the thrift. I shifted away from him, but not as far away as I would have liked. He breathed heavily through his mouth and stank of brine.

I doodled on my notepad, my own initials intertwined with realistic renderings of the prairie gentian. An ordinary girl would doodle her initials with someone else's, and intertwine them with hearts and roses, but in this awful, workaday world, I have come to realize that I can depend on no one but myself. As an experiment, I doodled Martin's initials with mine. As suitors go, he is parochial and clean, but the broad, offensive strokes of ML clashed with my delicate AP, so I scratched it all out immediately. How could I have a future with a man named Lemming? On the other hand, he likes to take me to nice restaurants, and the truth is, I have grown rather fond of it.

Tried not to let the Lemming occupy more of my brain. Mr. Genett described in excruciating detail a new project for us, composing and designing Web pages for the other departments. Depressing, as I have no interest in technology apart from solitaire.

He concluded with fake enthusiasm: "So by doing the work ourselves under present salary conditions, we can end the fiscal year for the National Association of Libraries in good shape." Mr. Genett, though possessed of a luxuriant head of hair, has the business acumen of Barney Fife. He had just announced to a roomful of underpaid servants that more work was to be heaped on, with no extra pay.

I looked around, expecting someone to protest, but everyone diligently wrote down the outline for the project and said nothing. So I did too. I am disgusted by our unthinking obeisance.

Mr. Genett then introduced the tech-support people who were going to teach us Web design and HTML coding. Two creatures entered the conference room. One resembled a sort of grasping stick-insect. A tangle of matted fur sprang from beneath a decaying baseball cap advertising RON'S PIZZA. He seemed permanently pitched forward at the waist, like a bent rake. The other I recognized as the tiny angry whale from the dungeon. He wore a black T-shirt that struggled to contain his bulk and a monstrous pair of black jeans. A thick mass of bristles jutted out from a moon face so pallid it made Coddles look positively tanned. The fluorescent lights in the conference room reflected off his oily globe of a head and dazzled me. A trail of perspiration oozed through the T-shirt, staining it white with salt.

"I'm Jeff," he said. "And this is the other Jeff. We'll be scheduling workshops over the next few weeks to teach you this stuff." Then he wiped his nose on the back of his hand, thus adjourning the meeting.

The bus journey home was no more enjoyable than the earlier voyage. The rain had not let up, and my umbrella finally gave out after years of halfhearted service. Its skeleton flapped open at the joints, as seemingly useless as a polio limb. But I found it still had a little zing in it after all, as I ground its tip into the insteps of fellow bus riders who trespassed on my personal space.

Approached my building with trepidation. The neighborhood urchins have made my plastic rain bonnet a point of attack. For once they were not lurking in the rubbish-strewn alley, so I took a quick look around, under the dead evergreen shrubs in the front, in the biohazard Dumpster from the mom-and-pop clinic on the corner, down the gangway between my building and the adjacent one. Nobody about, except for a lurching drunk emerging from the alley, so I felt it was all right to enter. Up the stairs to my apartment, I railed internally against the safety measures I must take to combat security risks. Once the urchins nailed me right in the head with an empty liter of Sprite, and old Paco from the first floor had to rush out and frighten them off. I laid on the front stoop in agony while Paco threw full cans of Busch beer at them. Barbaric times!

I threw down umbrella, bonnet, galoshes, and odious coat outside the door. Friday evening, but the pain of work had not yet released its hold. I hurried to the liquor cabinet and mixed myself a double tequila with lime. My roommate, Val Wayne, had guzzled all the vodka last week when he lost his job. Then we drank all the rum to celebrate his new job on Monday. I usually find tequila loathsome, but its bitterness seemed strangely appropriate today, with the rain and developments in the stinking job.

Phoned my mother and asked if she wanted me to come over for dinner on Sunday.

"I won't be available to cook," she said. "I'm going on a date."

"Well, you have to do whatever you think is best," I said.

She made an unintelligible snorting noise and told me to call Grandmother Prewitt for free eats. I resented the implication that I wanted to sponge food off my family. But Mother has an adder's tongue. Grandmother always said so.

I credit my grandmother with forming me into a presentable citizen. She exposed me to culture while my parents laid about on the floor all day. She taught me to cook decent food instead of that bulgur slop Mother always boiled up when she could be bothered to cook at all. Mother used to groan, "God, Addie, you're like a prison matron" when I ordered them out of bed for breakfast. Father would emerge from his marijuana hangover to chuckle at us, while I tidied their disgusting blankets and emptied the bong water.

Father used the weekends to recover from working, even though he was unemployed for the first nine years of my life. By "work" he meant staring into his potter's wheel, shaping wobbly bowls and dropping roaches in the clay. He sold a fair amount of gigantic ashtrays, though, and Mother had the marginally more conventional career of at-home seamstress, so we never starved. But our home was as filthy as a gypsy camp, and I fled to Grandmother's wholesome house down the street whenever possible.

I dialed up Grandmother, who naturally was overjoyed at the prospect of dining with me. She told me to invite the Lemming, but I knew he wouldn't want to go. He claims an allergy to chintz.

Before she rang off she said, "Addie, dear, why don't you bring that nice sherry we had last time? It was so delicious."

I promised I would, then made a mental note to soak the label off that old bottle of Strawberry Hill under the sink.

Topped off my tequila and rummaged around in our barren refrigerator for another lime. I found a ragged rind in the meat drawer and extracted what pitiful juice there was into the glass. Val likes to suck on limes as he relaxes on our revolting disco couch after a long day of work. I've warned him repeatedly about the effect of citric acid on tooth enamel, but he doesn't listen. His teeth are beginning to look like mossy stalactites, but he says, "So what? That's why I have a mustache."

Hope Mother enjoys herself on her date, selfish shrew, while I keep the old lady company. My father had been dead only three years when she decided to trash her respectable widowhood and prowl the gutters for men. Her current spousal equivalent is a philistine laborer called Jann. His accent is perfect South Side Chicago, but he looks like one of those heavy-handed Swedes. She claims Jann is an architect, but I've seen him lumbering about her apartment in a Bears jersey, and there's something about his massive shoulders that cries out for a yoke and harness. What kind of dates can they go on? All Jann likes to do is fish for crappie in Lake Calumet.

Curled up in the corner of the disco couch, averting my eyes from its grotesque geometric squiggles. At least it's comfortable, plus it was a bargain from Montgomery Ward's fire sale. I thought once I joined the walking dead in the work force, I'd be able to afford some finery and culture in my life, but the National Association of Libraries pays me only enough to live with a roommate and eat simple sandwiches.

Lionel Richie sang his classic "Hello" to me from the hi-fi, and I felt hot tears welling up. I wish a blind person would feel my face and make *me* a big clay head. Why is there no modern equivalent to Lionel? Today's music does nothing for me; the throbbing just gives me a peculiar feeling in the seat of my pants. Looked out the window. We on the third floor have a decent view of treetops, although they aren't in bud yet. It's early March, and as Grandfather used to say, it's not spring until it snows three times on the daffodils. We don't have daffodils here, but I'm marking the time by the snow on the biohazard Dumpster.

Val Wayne came home while I dozed on the couch. It was kind of him to tiptoe around as I slept, but I woke up when he tried to steal the lime wedge out of my drink. He had changed out of his shirt and tie to his usual household uniform of flared trousers and Black Sabbath baseball jersey. Lionel had been replaced on the stereo with something dark and menacing. I inquired as to the new paralegal job.

"Cinch," he said, stretching out in the Edith Bunker chair. It ranks a distant second in comfort behind the disco couch, but he punctured our beanbag chair at Christmas when a situation arose between a fondue fork and a jilted stenographer, and we haven't replaced it with anything yet.

"Want to order pizza?" he asked.

"I can't," I said. "The Lemming's coming to pick me up for dinner."

Val made a horrible retching sound which I chose to ignore.

"And where—"

I interrupted. "Blue Point Oyster Bar. Grilled amberjack with pecan sauce and julienned sweet potatoes. Two V&Ts before dinner, whatever wine he orders with the fish. Coffee. Key lime pie. And a to-go cup for the rest of the vodka."

Val stroked his mustache and nodded. He understands that after a childhood of eating kelp and sand and leaves with the parents, I need to eat quality meals more often than others of our miserable class.

"Help me find a frock?" I asked. He agreed and followed me into the closet in my bedroom. Val Wayne is all man, but he has impeccable taste in women's clothes.

I held a powder-blue velvet jumper with frilly cravat in front of me.

He shielded his eyes with his hand as though the sight caused him physical pain. "Ugh, you'll look more like Austin Powers than you already do." A comment directed at my buckteeth and occasional need for horn-rimmed spectacles.

"Right," I said, throwing it on the floor and selecting another. "How about this? Vintage nineteen-forties beige silk with white ruffled placket and darling little gloves to match."

"Again with the ruffles. What, are you having high tea with the count of Monte Cristo?"

He was ruthless, but I craved it, like a prize-fighter craves his corner man's insults. He nixed the black lace with mantilla ("bullfighter's widow"), the ice-blue twin set and pleated skirt ("librarian"), the green georgette crepe ("brown-noser at ladies' garden party"), and slightly stained pink organdy ("bedraggled slut"). He pushed me aside, dove in, and dredged up my champagne-colored sheath with silver lace overlay and ostrich feather hemline.

"Sexy yet oddball," he said. "The Lemming will act kind of embarrassed when you walk into the restaurant, but secretly he'll be into it."

I am uncertain if that's the reaction I'm looking for. Fending off the advances of a horny Lemming is a task too disgusting for words, but as my closet is so barren, I have no choice.

The rest of my toilette took only a minute, as I daresay I am young enough to go about fresh-faced with just a smear of lipstick. Emerged from the bathroom to present myself to Val. He asked if I'd been sprinkling arsenic on my cereal in the morning. Sometimes I find his cryptic comments annoying.

The doorbell rang promptly at eight, and I buzzed the Lemming in. Val quickly made himself busy at the hi-fi, throwing on his favorite Deep Purple album.

Martin Lemming looked his usual provincial self, boring black shoes, suit, white shirt, and rep tie. His strands of hair had been freshly laundered and parted an inch over his right ear. Let's call a spade a spade; he's balding. He also suffered an adolescent acne problem. It's all cleared up now, though when he leans in for a kiss I am forced to stare into the craters of fifteen-year-old pockmarks. In the Lemming's defense, I must admit that he is tall and virtually odorless. He is also the richest man I've ever known.

"Lemming," greeted Val.

"Val Wayne Newton," rejoined the Lemming. Val bristled at the taboo use of his full name. "Doing some hair farming?" Martin continued. "The 'stache is coming in nicely." I hurried the Lemming into the kitchen before fisticuffs broke out.

"Martin, darling," I breathed, kissing the air near one desperate-looking pit. "A drink?"

He chose a beer and struggled to twist off its cap. He has the smooth, milky fingers of an heir. My hands, I am sickened to note, are as gnarled as a harpy's claws, callused from the proletarian exertion of copyediting. I gulped another tequila as he appraised me like a choice rump roast. I shall never question Val's assessment of the power of the frock.

Martin shouted, "Ready to go?" over the third repetition of "Smoke on the Water." I nodded, filling up Grandmother's silver flask. As he downed the rest of his beer, complaining about our lack of recycling bins, I dashed about in search of a handbag to hold the flask. Luckily, I found my old rayon clutch under the disco couch. Score! I'd forgotten I left an airplane bottle of Tanqueray in it last year.

Said good-bye to Val, who was studying his mustache in the bathroom mirror.

"Hair farming," he muttered. "That pompous ass. He should rotate his own crops."

Agreed. If I could transplant the Lemming's nostril and ear fur to his scalp, he'd have hair as lush as a meadow of creeping phlox.

I told Val his mustache was really grand; he looked just like Lionel Richie midsize afro and all. He slammed the bathroom door in my face! I don't see why he should be so upset. Lionel Richie is one of the age's great balladeers.

I'm all for airplane bottles of gin. I never included Tanqueray in my repertoire before, but now that I've experienced the full effect of its properties, I shall make more room for it under the sink. Val threw a bottle of ginger brandy under there ages ago that can go in the rubbish when he's not looking.

Martin appeared mortified as I exited the car at the curb and tripped over my black velvet cape. He maintains that no one wears capes these days, but to me it's the obvious choice with silver lace and ostrich plumes. The wretched false Burberry is hardly appropriate.

I gave the hayseeds at the bar quite an eyeful. As Val Wayne had predicted, the Lemming propelled me over to a two-top in a dark corner, where he could ogle me in peace. As the drinks came, he launched into a dull monologue on superior restaurants in New York. The gin made it bearable.

When I'm with the Lemming, I find myself adding up his faults, weighing them against his advantages. I want to be sure I'm not wasting my time. His complexion is lumpy and variegated, and he doesn't get along with my best friend. Val in fact is my only friend and could not possibly be replaced with an oafish dullard like the Lemming. But I need to consider my future. Unless I am prepared for a lifetime of drudge labor, I will have to select a suitable husband. Martin is not, after all, hideously deformed. There is even a rakish attractiveness to his thin slot-mouth. He is intelligent and has conventional good taste. I agree with him on the principle of converting to an aristocracy, as long as they put me in the right class. You see, there is much to be said for our compatibility, as well as his tremendous stock portfolio.

If ever I falter in my resolve to marry the financially correct man, I need only summon the memory of my idiot father. He was too sensitive, with the artistic temperament so common to the *nouveau pauvre*. Only a frustrated potter would haul his family through the desolate dregs of this country in a ridiculous Volkswagen minibus for years, selling homeopathic remedies and singing songs. Disgusting! I was fifteen when he finally turned that hunk of junk toward home, but by then my sanity hung by a single flimsy thread.

Even though Mother has since taken up with the lumbering Swede, she claims to have warm memories of Father and his free-living ways. I say memories are fine for stuffing in silver picture frames, but they don't line the wallet or fill the dinner plates—even the misshapen ones the old man fired in the kiln. Mother still lives like a peasant. Only instead of trolling the commune and growing hydroponic rutabagas, she's tailgating Bears games and mending Jann's giant underpants.

"Two gin fizzes," Martin ordered after the plates had been cleared away.

I looked at the waitress. "That sounds good. I'll have the same."

"I suppose you want dessert," he said. I nodded enthusiastically.

"Well, we could share something," he murmured, perusing the dessert menu. Even though he's loaded, he can be shamefully tightfisted.

I frowned. "Why should I share when I can have one of my own?" Stupid Lemming. I pushed his floppy wrist off my thigh.

He let me eat my own slice of key lime pie while he visually gorged himself on my décolletage.

"You know, Addie," he breathed huskily, adenoids and all, "I love your clavicle."

I looked down at the slim little bone jutting out of my champagne sheath. I commented how nice a strand of matinee-length pearls would look cascading over it, but he just flailed for the waitress.

I escaped his clutches at my front door. I was not in the mood for a palsied tango, and anyway, his breath smelled like smoked chubs. I told him to order the Dover sole, but the chubs cost three dollars less.

Val Wayne was getting it on with one of his numerous lady friends on the disco couch. I have entered upon this scene so often that it fails to shock me anymore. He raised his head and asked how my evening went.

I elaborated on the vagaries of the seafood trade and the dressing up of fatty fish in general. Val agreed that no reasonable person should be forced to share one's dessert, no matter how much the meal cost. For a second I thought his playmate underneath gave me the ol' crook-eye, but I expect she was merely twitching in discomfort with her ankle way up there.

I retired to my bed, a worn-out husk. Dates with the Lemming can be so exhausting. But I suppose when we're married I'll learn to suffer his conversation and amorous groping, as do wives all over the world.

Turned on the radio to the inoffensive vocal standards station and read a dozen pages of Anthony Trollope before Val barged in.

"Heard the dentist music and wanted to come in and say good night."

"Lady friend gone?" I asked.

"Yeah." He sighed, sitting on the edge of the bed. "She got a charley horse and kicked me in the head."

Imagine getting a charley horse in the throes of passion! It lacks dignity.

"I heard you wrestling with the Lemming at the front door," he said. "Why don't you just give in?"

Involuntarily, I wrinkled my nose and frowned.

"Why no sex? I mean, he's repulsive, but you're so repressed, I think you need it."

"We have plenty of sexual tension," I replied. "He says my clavicle is his favorite part of my body."

Val agreed that my clavicle was my most attractive feature. But then Val has said I look like the skeleton hanging in our old high school biology lab.

"He's sure wasting a lot of money on you for nothing," he observed.

"Why do you think he takes me to all those nice restaurants?" I said. The Lemming is not without guile, but he has no idea what he's up against. I can hold out for years. He'll get his nauseating reward when he slips those four carats on my ring finger.

Val Wayne went to bed and I turned off the light. I laid there for ages, longing for sleep. My petty sexual dramas are a great source of hilarity for Val. Switched the radio station, looking for operatic love songs, but came upon the Metal Madness show. A song by Metallica assaulted me. Its rapid, pulsing bass line was a sound that usually sent me scrambling for my Neil Diamond records, but tonight it soothed me to sleep like a lullaby.

Chapter 2

Saturday passed in its usual dull fashion. I've outgrown the childish excitement that others feel for the weekend. For me it's just a break in the schedule, like when prisoners get sent out in the yard. Saturday night found me ironing sheets and rehemming my apron. Ever since they changed the stylish length of skirts this year, I've been forced to adapt my wardrobe. Val went to the movies with the tenants in 2F. He issued a weak invitation as he tied his shoes in the hallway, but I declined. The 2F boys have been snubbing me since they moved in last summer. I don't know why. I brought them a plate of sugar-free wheat-flour brownies as a housewarming present and was kind enough to warn them of the hazards presented by their mountain of work boots at the top of the stairs.

But once Sunday dawned I felt a thousand times better. Grandmother would be roasting a brisket and mashing potatoes while I poured out gallons of Strawberry Hill. I'm relieved that we don't have to dine with Mother. The last time she came with me to Grandmother's, she brought Jann uninvited. Grandmother said it was fine—that she would just run out to the store and pick up another roast beef, and for us not to worry about her; the snow had almost stopped. I thought that was very gracious of her, considering Mother just foisted the bullock boyfriend on us without a moment's notice. When it was time to eat, Grandmother insisted that Jann take the big comfy chair because she liked to stand while eating.

Mother had said, "For Christ's sake, Mother Prewitt." Grandmother smiled gently and put her fingertips to her temple, squinting a bit, and said she had a ripping headache, but for us to go on and eat while she laid down in the bedroom.

Mother slammed down her fork and roared, "Come on, Jann!" Then she stared at me as though I was supposed to get up and desert Grandmother and the brisket. The tension between us was as solid as the roast's antique salver, but the silence broke as she stomped out with the Viking in tow. Poor Grandmother emerged timidly from the bedroom a second later and sat down with me at the table. She picked up the fork Mother had thrown down.

"Reed and Barton," she sighed, fingering the engraving. "What a shame she bent the tines. It was a wedding present and all that I have left of your grandfather."

I reminded her that she had seventy-one other pieces in the set, but she just smiled sadly and shook her head, carving herself a tremendous slice of roast beef.

Thank God there would be no dramatic scenes at Gran's this time. My system is very delicate and can't properly digest amid emotional outbursts from the family. Frankly, I sometimes doubt my Anglo-Saxon ancestry when faced with the absolutely Sicilian theatrics that go on at family dinners.

Played my favorite Yanni album at top volume. It's a recording of his live concert at the Acropolis, the one where the music made Linda Evans cry. Soaked the label off the wine bottle. Val threw open his bedroom door and stumbled out into the kitchen. He wore silk boxers and a Styx T-shirt. His mustache was completely disheveled.

"It's nine in the morning," he groaned. Val sets aside Sunday mornings to recover from his hangovers, and dislikes when Yanni and I intrude. I think it's disgraceful how 2F always talks him into buying all the rounds at the Slavering Goat.

Val collapsed on the disco couch. Even though he abandoned me for 2F last night, I still felt a little sorry about his hangover, so I mixed him a Bloody Mary. We were out of Worcestershire; I used A-1 instead.

Weather was wretchedly cold but clear. The knockoff Burberry was defenseless against the wind. My teeth chattered on the El all the way up to Evanston, and an indecent old lech offered to warm me up with his rough workingman's hands. Revolting! The Red Line train usually attracts a better class of rider. I shall write a letter to the Chicago Transit Authority on office letterhead tomorrow to complain.

Grandmother's house is two stinking blocks from the El station, so I had to run in the cold all the way there. She has a yellow 1968 Valiant in her garage with four hundred miles on it and has never offered to pick me up. Once, in a snowstorm, I begged her for a ride back to the city, but she took so long to gather up her map, flares, CALL POLICE sign, pepper spray, lap rug, and thermos of mulled cider that I just left her in the garage and took the train.

A rush of happiness washed over me as Grandmother's house came into view. I always considered this home, instead of the mud and straw grotto my parents made us live in. Our house looked like one of Father's ill-formed bowls. My grandparents' house was refreshingly simple, with its cedar shingles and porch swing and clematis climbing up the arbor. If one considers this charming house or looks at old pictures of Father, one cannot deny that he was at some point a normal member of society. What could possibly have attracted him to Mother, or vice versa? The Prewitts said my parents met at a stock-car race where Mother lured strange men under the bleachers to smoke pot and feel around under her macramé vest. The Andersons said Father wandered into their yard one night and fell into the pool, high on jimsonweed. Whatever the truth, an attraction developed between them, Father embraced Mother's idle lifestyle, and a short time later she found herself preggers, sending them both into a descending paralysis from which neither ever recovered. I'm not proud of my humble origins, but there they are.

When I was born, Grandmother completely redecorated my father's old bedroom for me. It's still set up like that now, with white eyelet curtains and gingham sheets on the canopy bed, wallpaper with yellow irises, and bookshelves filled with Nancy Drew and photos of Father's old girlfriends. Mother turned *my* old bedroom into a workout center for Jann. He tosses dingy towels and jungle-patterned sports pants in the corner where my thin mattress once lay.

I greeted Grandmother in the kitchen, then hung my coat in the hall closet. Grandmother has a divine fox fur in there, sealed in a garment bag that has not been unzipped in nearly twenty years. When I was a little girl, my grandparents had a Christmas party. They invited all their geriatric friends and neighbors, and Mother, Father, and me. Cranky Aunt Jane refused to attend, as Father's patchouli always gave her a migraine. The parents came under duress, since that year they were railing about crass commercialism and oppressive Christian holidays. Driving over in our lousy rusted Volvo, Mother sulked in the passenger seat while Father jerked the broken steering wheel around.

"If they start in on us," Mother began to hiss, but Father cut her off with a meaningful look. I feigned ignorance while listening very carefully and playing with my homemade, genderless, non-race-specific doll.

He whispered, "They want to see Addie, and besides, Dad is lending us rent."

I'm sure my grandparents couldn't have been more pleased to see us traipse in an hour late, Mother draped in her wrath-of-God sari, hair hanging like two mangled jute cords from her flaky scalp, and Father drifting about in harem pants, his buttonless paisley tunic clasped in front by a small, crudely fashioned placard that read I DON'T BELIEVE IN YOUR GOD, BUT I'LL TAKE THE PRESENTS.

The elderly guests were polite and kind to us in spite of my parents' barnyard odor, probably because of my pretty pink party dress. It had been a birthday gift from Gran. Mother wanted me to wear a floor-length corduroy jumper, hemp kerchief, and peasant blouse, but I kicked and screamed for the frilly pink frock. Mother said, "If you want to look like Baby Jane Hudson, go ahead."

As was expected, the parents refused the roast beef and Yorkshire pudding. Mother said, "No flesh for us, thanks," and tore open her bag of unsalted organic tortilla chips. Father sipped tap water and ate Grandmother's green-bean casserole after blotting the vegetables with his napkin. I ate the roast as my parents looked on in disgust. I did not claw my way up the food chain to become an herbivore! Of course, now that she's slumming with that hulking boob Jann, Mother grills brats and burgers in the parking lot of Soldier Field. I've seen Jann sprinkle Bacon Bits on steak.

Anyway, after dinner Grandmother gave me my Christmas present, a pink fake-fur jacket. She put on her fabulous fox, and we modeled in front of the hall mirror by the closet. Mother's eyes bulged as Father attempted to restrain her, murmuring, "The rent, Ruth" in her ear. She said rent be damned, she could not endorse dead animals as clothing.

Grandmother said, "But it's only fun fur."

Mother said, "There is nothing *fun* about fur."

We left just about then. I had to keep my fun fur at Gran's house, since it was not *comme il faut* in our hut. Her own fox coat was put away in that garment bag, and I haven't seen her wear it since.

Had a fantastic dinner. Strawberry Hill goes well with everything. The only part that was a little wrenching was the dessert. She'd made a silver cake with seven-minute frosting, but it's obvious that she is getting to be ancient and sightless since I could see large strips of unmixed flour running through my slice. I did my best to choke it down; however, some of the flour went down the wrong tube and Grandmother had to thump me violently on the back.

I sputtered, "It's not the cake, Gran. It's my lungs, weakened from years of living with Val." It wasn't a lie, since his secondhand smoke had sent me racing from the room countless times and no doubt has damaged my vascular system.

We retired to the family room for tea. Grandmother brought out the tiny bottle of whiskey we sometimes use for flavoring and as a digestive aid.

Inevitably, she brought up the cursed subject of work. I try to keep a brave face when speaking of the Place, as I've come to call it, to Grandmother. It was she, after all, who paid for my college education, and I feel the need to reassure her that I've put my schooling to good use. To confide that all college provided me with was the skill to differentiate good beer from poor beer would crush her—especially to hear that I spent whole weekends slogging down inferior, trail-of-cat-sick brew! She would also hate to know how I detest my job. Anyway, it was easy to steer her back to safer territory. March in the suburbs means ordering seeds and plants for spring, and getting the earth ready for gardening. Her perennial bed was unrivaled in the neighborhood, and I always enjoyed working on it, even though too much fresh air makes me nauseous. She let me prattle on about cabbage worms and black spot and earwigs while she fiddled with the whiskey decanter.

"Tea's not very strong," she commented, upping the whiskey-to-tea ratio to halvsies.

"Shall we order Sugar Daddy snap peas again?" I asked. I found this hilarious, considering my dalliance with the Lemming.

"Addie, I believe I won't be planting anything new this year," she said. She pulled an invisible thread from a petit point sofa pillow. I listened in shock to her litany of physical complaints: rheumatoid arthritis, failing eyesight, fallen arches, leaky bladder. Nothing could persuade her to dig in the dirt this summer.

It was like hearing that your priest consulted a psychic hotline, or that Abraham Lincoln preferred drunken carousing to books. The rose pruning and training of the trumpet vines of the past now seemed meaningless, empty, unreal.

"The clematis?" I gasped, struggling to keep my emotions under control.

She shrugged—a vulgar gesture in a lady of her age.

"Is everything just going to rack and ruin in your yard, then?" I demanded, voice quaking.

"Well, the boy next door is a horticulture major at Northwestern. He said he'll do some weeding and pruning."

My world, pedestrian void that it is, came crashing down around me. All that had gotten me through the endless winter months of editing academic drivel, eating stale crusts in the staff cafeteria, staring out my apartment windows at naked trees with plastic bags stuck in the branches, enduring moronic conversations with the Lemming, slumping in my folding chair at the Place, had now disappeared with one selfish utterance of an old woman.

I stood up, trembling. What was I to do with spring and summer now? Chase the tamale vendors throughout my neighborhood? Tan in a sleazy bikini on the fire escape? Stand in the alley with the other vagrants and mongrels, eating discarded corncobs and drinking rainwater?

"Oh, dear," said Grandmother. She patted my arm. Valiantly, I told her it was all right, that ripping the garden away from me would free up time to forge a closer bond with Mother and Jann. Grandmother's lips narrowed to one cruel, thin line, but she said nothing.

I asked if I could have a few moments to bid farewell to the perennial bed and compost heap. She sighed mightily and nodded, and I was uncomfortably reminded of my father, who sighed in much the same manner when I left the paper open to the Help Wanted section near his cereal bowl.

Grandmother bundled up in her winter coat and followed me outside. My torment at leaving our beautiful garden untended this season was matched only when the icy wind tore through my blasted coat.

There was nothing much to say good-bye to yet. It was too early to see any real green growth. I just stared at the pine mulch and bawled.

"Don't wail out here in the yard, before prying eyes," she admonished, casting about for spying neighbors. "It's inappropriate to become excited outdoors."

I wiped my tears and moaned softly, in a pretty, feminine way.

"Wait!" Grandmother shouted. She shuffled over to the garage and picked something off the old potting bench. "Here, take this," she said, pressing something into my hand. Hoping it was cash, I was disappointed to find it was a packet of red salvia seeds.

"Thanks," I gulped, stuffing the package into my coat pocket. Again tears sprang to my eyes; red salvia is the ugliest flower in cultivation.

Foul mood by the time I got back home. From out on the sidewalk I heard the strains of "Smoke on the Water." Paco from 1F stood in the hallway, wearing a red velour jogging suit, socks, and plastic sandals. He's an old immigrant, so he cannot be expected to know our American styles. I'm not sure where he came from originally. There are some ridiculous-looking pen-and-ink marks on his mailbox that might be

Greek or Chinese or Russian, but everyone calls him Paco. He answers readily enough.

Paco looked searchingly up the stairs and asked where all the noise came from. I blamed 2F.

Up in our apartment, Val Wayne strummed his guitar along with the music. His eyes were closed and he clenched a cigarette butt between his lips, endangering his mustache. I'm all for music, heaven knows I've spent many evenings rocking out to the Ray Conniff Singers, but Val's musical tastes offend me. I turned down Deep Purple and threw my raincoat on the floor like a common street thug.

"What's your problem?" he asked, turning up the music. We stood at the stereo controls, poised like dogs at a standoff. As usual, I capitulated. I begged Val for a turn at the record player, explaining that my grandmother had severed my sanity with one final snip of her floral shears, and that only consolation from Lionel or Neil or Abba or Yanni could restore me. Coldhearted, he refused!

Tried to cry, but Val has known me since I was fifteen and can see through the thin veneer of my tears. We have had many arguments over the years about Deep Purple, and "Smoke on the Water" in particular, but I cannot sway him to reason. He always ends our debate by saying that I will never understand what those four chords have meant to him.

Nothing is more depressing than bathing while Deep Purple chugs on into the night, but as the loser in the stereo battle—as in so many others—I had no choice. I filled up the old claw-foot tub and added a few drops of attar of roses. It doesn't take much rose-scented steam to permeate this empty shell of a girl. Afterward, I padded around in white fuzzy slippers and a high-necked muslin nightgown, filing my nails into sharp points.

As is Val's usual Sunday-night ritual, he combed out his mustache at the bathroom mirror and measured its growth with a ruler.

"It's not growing." He pouted. I went in to have a look. I said it looked longer to me, but I was only being kind. Val's mustache has not changed in three years.

"It doesn't grow past the corners of my mouth," he said, showing me the smooth hairless patch by his lips. I pointed out that only Lynyrd Skynyrd roadies grew mustaches longer than his.

"I know," he replied with despondent envy.

He groomed himself a while longer while I went into the bedroom to select my outfit for work tomorrow. After a quick consultation with the Weather Channel and the Farmer's Almanac, I chose a cherry-red wool-blend gabardine dress with starched white collar and antique enamel buttons. Gray cashmere cardigan (Grandmother's hand-me-down), nude hose, gray loafers. The effect was unfortunately librarianish, but with red lips and no Kleenex in the sleeve, I could take my place within the current century. I had no one I wanted to impress at the Place, but there was always the chance that some Wall Street tycoon would ride the bus if his roadster was in the shop. Hung the dress on the closet door and readied the accoutrements on the chair. Also set aside the plastic rain bonnet with charming red trim and hung up the fake Burberry, which I had thrown on the floor, after first polishing its D-rings and belt buckle and brushing out its useless lining. Val was *still* fussing with his mustache in the bathroom! Who could possibly be attracted to someone of such fastidious habits?

Laid in bed and felt the sniffles coming on. Blasted Gran! Tried to feel sorry for her collapsing health, but it was no good. She *could* have insisted I come over three times a week to fix up the garden, like the old days, but I guess she just prefers to lie about the house all day, watching her yard degrade into a rubbish heap. How long will it be before she has the fancy floral student from next door drag out the Valiant to rust on the front lawn, propped up on cinder blocks? A splitting headache was upon me now. I toyed with the idea of calling in sick tomorrow, but those of us treading the poverty line have to press on with work in spite of illness. I felt that I understood how Polish laborers in the munitions factories of World War II felt before commencing eighteen-hour workdays shod only in ill-fitting, thunderous work boots. My own loafers pinched mightily at the toes.

At the Place, a workshop had been scheduled for us copyeditors and the graphic designers. The two Jeffs herded us into a dank cave around the corner from the dungeon. This was the tech-support department, known as the Hole throughout the rest of the building. Windowless, with naked fluorescent bulbs running the length of the room, the Hole was separated from nontech staff by a wall of plate glass and a locked glass door. A frail administrative geek sat Cerberus-like at a desk outside the door to keep out trespassers. As though we respectable aboveground workers would want to mix with the subterranean techies!

Opened my notebook at the beginning of the training session. Wrote down silly tech terms. Felt sleepy. I had not anticipated so much information. The Jeffs took turns explaining the software program and demonstrating techniques on the computer. I felt they could have gone to a little more trouble to clean themselves up before the meeting. It was very distracting trying to concentrate on the monitor while the fat, bald Jeff sweated through his T-shirt. The grasshopper-looking Jeff was no easier on the eyes, as his filthy ropes of fur swung to and fro beneath the moldy RON'S PIZZA cap, dislodging crumbs and invertebrates every few seconds. Coddles attended the workshop for two minutes, just to make sure we all showed up. Then he left to gather up his dry cleaning for the secretary to drop off.

Bev and Lura took copious notes. The graphic designers seemed to have some prior knowledge of this HTML thing and didn't need much of a tutorial. I was the only one struggling to understand. I have decided that when the time comes for me to format a website, I shall have to sever some wires within my hard drive and pass the job on to someone else.

We broke up into small groups to practice what we had learned. In my group were tartar Bev and one of the graphic designers. He is called Francis and looks like he's worn the same pumpkin-farmer jeans for a month straight. He had some foreign matter in his hair, but I was not about to reach in. I tapped him on the shoulder with my Bic and pointed wordlessly to the clump of refuse on his head. He felt around gingerly, then extracted a Cheerio. He didn't say anything, but he looked grateful as he popped it into his mouth.

Bev insisted that I go first and attempt to format a simple sentence and a block of color. I stared at the screen for an instant, then starting pressing keys. My group exchanged glances.

"Have you ever worked on a computer before?" asked Francis.

Relieved, I said he should take his turn and gave him a dazzling smile for encouragement. He cringed and turned toward the machine. Subsequent furtive glances in my compact told me I still had great clumps of spinach omelet in my bucks.

Bev looked quite pleased with herself after my disastrous performance. She told me to pay attention because if I didn't learn it now, I would never get it. I responded that those of us with youth still on our side were better equipped to acquire new skills. Her nostrils flared aggressively and a hard line appeared between her brows, but she kept quiet. Round one to me.

Something strange I noticed during the session: our trainers are referred to as Fat Bald Jeff and Other Jeff by the rest of the tech-support staff. They don't seem to be insults— merely accepted names. Even their supervisor interrupted our workshop and said, "Fat Bald Jeff, there's a printer crisis on the fourth floor in accounting when you're done here."

After an hour in the Hole, I felt I could stand no more. There were too many tech workers and not enough deodorant. My nasal cavities are very sensitive and cannot take repeated doses of human stench. The desks were strewn with Coke cans and moldy candy bar wrappers. The wall above Fat Bald Jeff's personal workstation boasted an old poster of

William Shatner. Someone had mangled an ancient 5¼" floppy disk and hammered it to a crucifix made from company pencils. The floor was littered with debris fallen from mangy beards.

Finally, the Jeffs released us. The others looked over their notes by the stairs while I waited for the elevator. I wished that I, too, could have escaped into the stairwell, but I'm susceptible to labored breathing and have to be careful not to overtax my lungs. At the last minute, Fat Bald Jeff squeezed his bulk into the elevator with me. My final view before the doors closed was of Bev's smug pig face, framed by iron-gray bangs and outdated Peter Pan collar. She made disparaging clucking noises and said, "Elevator for only two floors up? My, my." Of course the doors shut before I could reply.

After a moment, Fat Bald Jeff said: "Why walk when you can ride?"

It seems we are not so different after all.

Spent the whole afternoon composing smart retorts to Bev's insolent and not very witty barb. I waited for her to comment again on the elevator so I could announce, "Stairs are for peasants," but she completely ignored me the rest of the day. I did, however, feel a small gratification when she left the ladies' room with her horrible denim skirt tucked into her mammoth pantyhose. It was a disgusting sight, but one I enjoyed nevertheless.

Edited the unspeakably dull article "Amassing Aggregations for the Online Library Reference Center." I must be absolutely brilliant because I was able to edit the whole manuscript without once looking up the meaning of "aggregations." It must mean mobs of angry people, but why would libraries want to amass them? It's not my problem; I'm just the copyeditor. Challenged the computer to a little solitaire. It won.

Left work at four-thirty. The day is not officially over until five, but I felt after all I had been through with Grandmother and the new duties in our department, I deserved a reprieve. Hid in the company coat closet until Coddles shut his office door for a meeting with his slutty secretary, Miss Fernquist. When no one was looking, I tiptoed down the hallway and took the stairs slowly down one floor to the exit. This is just how spies must feel when tailing international terrorists. I've got to say, it was thoroughly exciting. I can't describe the thrill I had on the sidewalk, looking at my wristwatch and seeing the minute hand sweep the half hour! Of course, the thrill disintegrated when I was reminded of the inferior quality of the watch. Why not just strap a stone sundial to my head and sheep bladders on my feet? I am completely outmoded.

Strolled past the little frock shop I adore on Oak Street, coveting the spring line displayed in the front window. Like a starving beggar child in Victorian England pressing its nose against a bakery window, I pressed my nose against the shop glass. The day was gray and windy, and trash adhered to my legs as it blew down the street. The most darling petal-pink Empire sheath with décolleté bodice hung mere inches from me, but for all my meager finances it might have hung on top of the John Hancock building. A saleslady appeared on the other side of the window, glaring at me with frank disapproval. I moved slowly toward the bus stop, making little sad sounds. I wanted that dress: it was a grown-up version of the one Gran gave me all those years ago. But if I bought it, I would have to forgo all new purchases and decent groceries for eight months. I suppose I should have been used to squalor by now, but I couldn't help rebelling against enforced penny-pinching and egg salad sandwiches. My parents were never plagued by this longing for quality wardrobe, but then good breeding sometimes skips a generation.

It's so destructive to pity oneself. Ugly lines form at the corners of one's mouth that only a Lynyrd Skynyrd mustache could disguise. As I walked, I tried to rally. Just think of the starving Victorian children, forced to work as scullery maids and bootblacks. I wouldn't last two minutes as a scullery maid; my arms are too thin and feeble to haul in coal from the scuttle, not to mention the number it would do on my bronchial tubes. All for a lice-infested blanket and bowl of thin gruel. My digestion is extremely testy and cannot handle gruel. No, with my constitution I would have been much better suited to the life of the chronically ill Victorian lady, coughing delicately into a Battenburg lace hanky while servants remarked on my courage.

Pink is my color. Everything else makes me look gaseous. Of course, only Gran realized this . . . Mother made me child-labor uniforms in various corpselike shades. The pink dress Gran gave me for my ninth birthday was spectacular, with its puffed sleeves, daring Empire waist, and flowing knee-length skirt. She and Grandfather brought it over to our house, and I ran to my room to try it on immediately. The grandparents clapped as I twirled around, while the parents snickered, natch, calling me Prissy Princess. They preferred me in sackcloth and ashes.

Gran said, "Doesn't she look like little Eliza Doolittle? After Rex Harrison transformed her, of course."

Huge argument ensued, with parents defending Eliza's right to talk bad and dress in dirty frocks.

Gran sniffed, dabbing at her eyes with a monogrammed hanky, explaining that she only wanted to do something nice for her granddaughter, heaven knows she couldn't do much, and she would just stay out of their lives if that's what they wanted. I clutched Gran's skirt fiercely and glared baby poison darts at my parents.

Father apologized lamely while Mother prayed to Krishna for strength. Gran squinted and touched her temples. She said she had a sudden migraine and would just wait out in the car for Grandfather.

"Oh, Christ!" spat Mother, stomping into the bedroom and slamming the door.

"Oh, gee," said my father, biting his cuticles and looking back and forth between Grandfather and me.

Grandfather patted me on the head and said, "Addie, you don't have to admire Eliza Doolittle if you don't want to."

I said, "I admire Lizzie Borden."

Grandfather went to his car, I gazed at my reflection in the mirror, and Father ran out to lock the tool shed.

Chapter 3

New development with 2F: I was vacuuming the hallway before work one morning this week when the door to their apartment swung open. A voice called out to tell Jadwiga, the janitoress, to knock it off until after noon. I replied that it was not Jadwiga, who usually can be found eating salami in the laundry room and *not* vacuuming, but Addie Prewitt, 3R. I looked over the railing as the owner of the voice looked up the stairs. I met the gaze of an Asian gentleman in silk pajamas with a black satin eyeshade pushed up on his forehead.

"Hello, Mr. Chung," I called gaily. He made an odd, guttural noise and flapped his arm slightly in greeting. Progress! As he turned back to his apartment, I caught a glimpse of a Turkish rug fringe inside the entryway, and a stack of empty liquor bottles five feet high. I am intrigued. Perhaps I have misjudged 2F by their occasional pile of lumpen work boots.

That day the sun shone its first feeble rays. The sky had broken up in pieces, clouds parted to admit custard-colored light. No green growth yet, but the alleys sported fresh puddles of vomit, a sure sign of spring in our neighborhood. A line of diseased individuals with crying children had already formed outside the mom-and-pop clinic. Snow had melted on the biohazard Dumpster. Paco swept up the broken glass on the sidewalk in front of our building while his wife, a sullen giantess in an orange muumuu, glowered at him from their front windows.

Even at the Place I felt loads lighter. No demanding zombies lurched into my cubicle all morning. I took a break from proofreading the galleys for the thrillsville journal *Technical Services Quarterly* to stare out my cubicle window. We in the publishing department have cubicles lined up against the windows. Plenty of other peons in the building merely face other cubicle partitions. The Place itself is U-shaped, with a parking lot and garbage heap in the courtyard area we can look down upon. I am grateful for my cubicle window, even if the Place resembles an office version of *Rear Window.* Except that I have never seen anything as exciting as Raymond Burr murdering his wife.

I heard Coddles stumping down the hallway, making feeble introductions.

"This is uh, ahem . . . our new temp. He'll be helping out around here as you work on the Web project." A harassed-looking young man followed, nodding absently to each cubicle resident as he passed. Coddles stuck the temp at a workstation in the middle of the common area, where the printer, copy machine, and joyless secretaries sit. How unfeeling and automated our work society has become when the temps don't even get their own cubicles. There were still two hours to go until lunch, so I took some company stationery out of the supply closet and composed a stern letter to the Chicago Transit Authority. It read:

Dear Sir or Madam:
I am writing in regard to the harrowing experience I endured last Sunday as I rode the Red Line to visit my sick grandmother. I quietly sat, awaiting my stop to

switch over to the Evanston Express, when a disgusting fellow passenger made a most indecent and improper advance toward me! (It took fifty minutes from the Loop—that's ten minutes longer than usual. Are your conductors adequately trained? It shouldn't be that difficult, pushing the Go lever and pulling the Stop.) I suggest you place armed guards, or at least those Hells Angels with the red berets, in each car from now on, or I will cease my CTA business travel immediately! I have the full support of my organization behind me!

Sincerely,
Coddles

I had written several drafts before this using my own name, but they didn't seem to carry the weight that middle management did. Even Coddles's e-mail address rings with more authority than mine. It uses his name (a.barr@nla.org) in the address, unlike mine, which just uses my cubicle position (prod.3@nla.org). I penciled his e-mail address under his name, sealed the letter in an envelope, and dropped it in the mailroom guy's cart—the Place can afford first-class stamps for my infrequent personal letters. Francis, the soiled graphic designer, and Bev informed me that the Jeffs had scheduled another HTML training session for our little group. This really disrupted my day, as I prefer to eat lunch at 12:05 exactly and would now have to put off the meal for at least another hour. I patiently explained to them about my digestion and how its healthful function depends on a rigorous eating routine that varies by not even one instant.

Bev said, "This gives 'anal retentive' a whole new spin," and the plebe Francis burst out laughing. I said nothing as they stood around enjoying themselves at my expense. If there is a God, then perhaps he is taking note of this spectacle and making marks in a specialized booklet.

Suffered through another workshop. I've lost all hope of catching up and have now decided to spend these occasions in the Hole making ironic observations about the techies. While Bev and Francis jot down inane instructions from the Jeffs, I record my thoughts in my notebook. I have noticed, for example, that while all the tech hobbits defer to Fat Bald Jeff on everything from system configuration to take-out menus, they regard Other Jeff as an irritating speck of lint. Poor Other Jeff . . . he's quite harmless, but he does seem to bumble around a lot for someone in charge of network administration. Their supervisor came in and disrupted our session to ask Other Jeff why he had left his (the supervisor's) Mont Blanc in a cup of coffee on the desk. Other Jeff explained nervously that he thought that the supervisor left his pens in a coffee mug.

"Not a full one, dumb-ass," barked the supervisor. "Next time use your brain, if there *is* one trapped under that stupid baseball cap."

The Hole occupants snickered at Other Jeff, and for a moment I felt I could empathize with him, having recently been made a laughingstock myself by hag Bev and Francis. But Other Jeff lifted his RON'S PIZZA cap for a second to adjust his fur, and the sight of all those burrs and snarls relieved me temporarily of human feeling. Fat Bald Jeff, however, ceased his instruction. He took an imposing step toward the techies and fixed upon them the ferocious stare of the angry baby whale, just like when he assaults the pastry platter in the morning.

"Is there something funny?" he bellowed. The techies glanced around sheepishly at one another, laughter dying all around. They turned to their workstations, backs curling up tightly like boiled prawns. Satisfied that the message went through, Fat Bald Jeff smiled rather grimly and came back to our astonished little group. Other Jeff looked down at Fat Bald Jeff with submissive gratitude. Fat Bald Jeff nodded shortly in response and resumed the lesson. Strange! It would never pass muster aboveground, but in the Hole it pays to be Fat Bald Jeff.

At the end of the session, the Jeffs gave us a sample assignment to work on later in our cubicles. Francis tried to peek at my notebook as we packed up to leave.

"How's it going? Need any help?"

I assured him that all was under control. As if I wanted a graphic delinquent hanging about my desk in his scandalous pumpkin pants and potato-digging fingernails. A girl has to maintain some standards in her cubicle. The indignity of no door is bad enough without inviting the rabble in.

Faint with hunger by the time I reached the elevator. Steady on. I waited, leaning against the wall for support as Bev hoisted her elephantine ankles up the stairs. She looked back over her dowager's hump at me, wearing a superior expression. I had no energy to parry with her over my use of the elevator. Practically fell out the doors at the second floor and crawled into the staff lounge. Opened the refrigerator door to retrieve my sack lunch. *Gone!*

Frantically, I searched the fridge, every shelf, every dusty egg bin, every moldy crisper. The brown bag was nowhere.

"My lunch is gone! My lunch is gone!" I screamed, running out into the common area. I was trembling with rage and low blood sugar. The temp woke up and the secretaries looked over, mildly annoyed.

"Someone has stolen my lunch! I must sit down," I gasped. I tried to lower myself into a chair at the conference table but misjudged the distance and fell down. Of course, sniggering all around.

The graphic designers' cubicles were just opposite the common area, and the three of them strolled out to watch the show. Francis, at least, had the good manners to help me up and into the chair while his vile colleagues stood there and rubbernecked.

"Someone has stolen my lunch," I repeated to Francis, who sat next to me at the table. "I feel dizzy." I blinked, and two big tears plopped down.

"What was in your lunch?" he asked. "Maybe somebody grabbed it by accident. There's always so many bags in the fridge."

My voice shook as I recited the contents. "Tofurkey tarragon with Danish havarti, butter, and radicchio on seven-grain millet bread. One banana, cubed. Pepperidge Farms' Distinctive Milano cookies, two."

He looked as though he was fighting the urge to smile. I don't see what's so hilarious about the theft of one's food. He asked the other graphics fellows as well as Lura and Bev about the missing lunch. Bev came out to the common area with a toothpick working its way through her decayed brown fangs.

"All this fuss over a cheese sandwich?" she crooned. Francis had to restrain me, which wasn't too difficult given my weakened state.

"How come you put cheese *and* butter on the sandwich?" asked one of the graphic designers.

"Yeah," said the other. "Wouldn't cheese and all the other junk be enough?"

Junk! That pound of sliced tofurkey cost $7.98! Not to mention the expense of organic radicchio, which has a rather unpleasant texture but wonderful color.

I screamed, "The point is, it was *stolen*, simpletons! We have a thief in the building, ripping sandwiches out of the mouths of the hungry." Slowly, all eyes came to rest on the temp, who was nervously sharpening pencils.

"It wasn't me," he said in a small voice.

Lura spoke up quickly. "Now, let's not make any accusations. Addie, I have a sandwich I'll split with you. Come into my cubicle." She pulled me up and dragged me out of the common area around the corner.

We sat down as she split up the contents of her lunch on the desk. I wiped my tears and exhaled a quivering breath. At least someone at the Place had a little consideration. I did my best to smile at this one kind soul through my anguish and peristalsis. She smiled back as she pushed over half of her ham sandwich.

I sniffed it. "Is this white bread? Because I really try to avoid it. It's so bad for you."

A strange expression crossed her face. She probably had never heard about the digestive pitfalls of processed flour.

"Well, I suppose one time won't hurt," I said, taking a tiny bite.

After lunch, I took a brisk walk around the block to calm my nerves. It exhausted me. To have to go back in the midst of my laughing coworkers, one of whom is a remorseless criminal, was too much to bear. At least Lura was a decent sort, generous to me in my time of need. Back in my cubicle, I looked warily out the window at the thousand windows opposite me. A thieving madman roamed those corridors—but who? Where?

"Everything all right?" I jumped at the sound of a voice behind me.

Oh, it was just Francis. I nodded and turned away. The thief was probably not him, as he usually ate greasy fried flesh with his colleagues each day. On the other hand, he always appears to be on the verge of scurvy and perhaps felt the need for a healthful meal.

"Have you been in this cubicle long?" he asked, glancing around.

"Four years," I responded.

"Wow," he said. "It looks like nobody even works in here."

A comment directed toward my lack of office decoration. I like to keep my cubicle as barren as a spinster's lingerie drawer. Everyone else in the department has plants, posters of kittens on ropes begging you to "hang in there," and photos of loved ones. I may be resigned to the idea that I am toiling myself into an early grave, but I have no desire to fool myself into thinking of the Place as home.

"I have to work on the sample Web page," I finally said to Francis as he stood there gawking at my blank walls.

He sighed and walked back to his side of the wing. His sigh was irritated, but I expect it's just that he, too, is dreading the boring project. The Jeffs had handed us each a sheet of gibberish, detailing what we were to do. I read it over for a moment, then checked the corridor to see if anyone approached. Then I unplugged the computer and opened up the back of the hard drive. I cut a wire with an X-Acto knife—easy enough! But I couldn't get the back panel of the machine on again. Finally I found an old Zero candy bar in my desk and shoved that in there, too. Its gooey, melting icing would seal the box up nicely. I felt a twinge of regret afterward, when I realized I had thus incapacitated the solitaire game as well.

I knew I had to behave as normally as possible—the usual course of action when one's computer conks out is to plead for help from tech support—so I took the elevator down to the Hole. I tried to walk past the desk geek at the glass door, but he laid a dry paw upon my arm, barring my way.

"Sorry. You can't just waltz into tech support."

"But my computer's broken," I said. "I need to alert the proper authorities."

"I'll page somebody," he said.

"But they're all sitting right there," I said, annoyed. "Can't I just knock on the door?"

The desk geek looked aghast. "You most certainly cannot. Who worked on your machine last time this happened?" I gulped. Do they really keep track of these things? I had dismantled the computer once last year. A greedy co-worker had taken a few additional days of maternity leave, and Coddles forced extra editorial duties upon me. People can be so selfish.

"Um, it was Jeff," I lied.

The desk geek drew in a long breath and fluttered his eyelids rapidly. "Which one?"

"Fat Bald, Fat Bald," I replied quickly.

He droned into the intercom system. "Fat Bald Jeff, please come to the administration desk. Fat Bald Jeff, to the administration desk."

The stout little man answered the page immediately and listened intently as I explained the problem.

"I see," he said finally. "You turn the machine on, yet nothing happens. Is that right?"

I nodded. We then walked to the elevator together. As it spat us out on the second floor, Jeff stepped into the pale sunlight streaming in through the hall windows and blinked as if in pain. I was reminded again of the sea and imagined Jeff as a sightless albino fish swimming around in a dark cave all its life, never once seeing the sun.

"So bright up here," he complained. I replied that, yes, March sunlight in Chicago is often brutal, but my sarcasm went unnoticed.

We entered my cubicle and I sat in my folding chair as Fat Bald Jeff manhandled the computer.

"I guess I won't be able to finish that sample project you gave us this morning," I said.

He shrugged. "You'll have to take that up with Coddles. I'm just the trainer."

I detested the idea of willingly entering Coddles's office, but I felt it was my duty to slip out of this assignment as quickly as possible so he could give the work to someone else. I knocked on his door and went in. He was wedged tightly behind his yucko Louis XIV desk, emptying the contents of a Chinese take-out carton into his mouth. The remains of a sub sandwich lay ravaged at his elbow. His hair, if one can call a slick strand grown to the length of five feet and wrapped several times around the head "hair," must have fallen into the carton recently, as it dripped brown MSG goo all over Coddles's dandruff-flaked shoulders. He held up a pudgy finger, indicating that I should wait while he licked the inside of the container clean.

When Caligula had finished gorging himself, I told him about my computer and my inability to complete the assignment.

He said, "Oh, that Jeff will have your computer up and running in no time." I allowed myself a wry, knowing smile.

"However," he continued, "you might as well make yourself useful while he fixes it. Here."

He handed me a ticket stub and told me to go pick up his dry cleaning! I stared at him in shock. Was I now reduced to valet status? Correction: not even valet; this was clearly the humble task of the *third footman*.

"What's wrong?" he asked. I could not even articulate my objection. "Oh," he said after a moment. "You'll need money." And he withdrew a grubby bill from his nether regions.

Feeling the bile rise up from the combination of menial chore, Coddles's touch, and ham-on-white, I pocketed the cash and ran out of his office.

"Don't forget the change," he called after me.

I paused at my cubicle to rally. Facing me from beneath the computer desk was Jeff's massive "plumber's crevice." Deliver me, Lord!

I cleared my throat. "I have to step out for a moment. Coddles wants me to pick up his dry cleaning." Fat Bald Jeff sat back on his considerable haunches and sighed. A greasy film covered his bulbous forehead. Dark rings formed at the armpits of his black T-shirt. His Levi's strained at the thighs.

"That's all right," he said, mopping his brow with a bandanna. "I have to run back down to tech support. I'm going to need tools."

This was an ominous decree, but I was not displeased. It foretold endless hours of not working on the Web project while Fat Bald Jeff tinkered inside my computer, muttering, "What's *this* for?" and smashing things. The unpleasant picture it drew of a sweating, irritable Jeff defying the power of his deodorant was worth the time it would free up for me at the Place.

The address on the ticket stub took me several blocks from the Place (curse you, Coddles) to a tailor/cleaner that I myself have patronized in the past. The tailor was a swarthy rascal I called "the Little Frenchman," though there was something of the menacing Middle East about him. Truthfully, I'm not sure from whence he came, but—like the French— he speaks as though his mouth is stuffed with muffins. Anyway, one dusky foreigner is much like another.

Although my old gray loafers were in need of minor cobbling and inappropriate for so much exercise, I rather enjoyed the heartiness of a spring walk. Grandmother and I used to walk the perimeter of her yard this time of year with notebook in hand, jotting down ideas for the perennial bed, noting which shrubs needed pruning, laughing at the hideous birdbath given to her by my parents many years ago. In the center, it bore a large, smiling she-frog wearing a bun hairdo and spectacles just like Grandmother's.

"Mother picked it out," I had told her, but she said she had already guessed that. Mother's taste has always been shockingly plebeian.

The thought of Grandmother and the garden gave me a peculiar twinge. Not quite anger, but a kind of vague sorrow. This type of emotional contemplation can only set the digestive juices flowing the wrong way, so I quickly shut it from my mind.

I handed the Little Frenchman the ticket. He returned with the garments, and I was grateful for the protective plastic bag that separated my skin from their fibers. I had no desire to touch any fabric that had ever rubbed against Coddles's coarse flesh.

The Little Frenchman winked at me. "They are for your husband, no?" I sent poison darts shooting from my eyes.

"*Au contraire,* they belong to my boss," I explained, lest even one insignificant person on this planet think that I willingly coupled with Coddles.

He shrugged, handing me back the change and a sealed envelope. "Items he left in the pocket. I don't want," he said, as though he would be entitled to keep anything he found that he did want.

I walked back toward the Place. I hoped that when I returned, Fat Bald Jeff would be weeping and sitting on the wreckage from my disemboweled computer, warranting me an early leave today. With some of the change from the Little Frenchman, I bought myself a lemonade at the Italian café next door to work. As I waited for the Italian behind the counter to properly crush the ice (I had to send it back twice), I looked at the sealed envelope in my hand. I thought, Why not? I could easily replace the envelope with a blank one from the supply closet, and Coddles would never know the difference.

So I ripped it open. With interest, I removed a creased and sticky magazine photo of a plump, naked woman holding a martini glass under one droopy breast and leering walleyed in the general vicinity of the camera. I stared at the picture for some time, taking in its ample, disgusting value.

"Ma'am?" shouted the soda jerk, loudly enough to make everyone else at the counter turn to look at me. He saw the picture and smirked, handing me the lemonade. I wanted to correct him, as I am obviously youthful enough to be called "Miss," but he continued to stare as I fumbled with the money and pornography, so I just left without a word. I think I will write a letter to his superiors.

Back on the second floor, I hesitated by the corner of our hallway. I caught a glimpse of Fat Bald Jeff tapping his hoof outside my cubicle. He looked rather agitated. But as I had nowhere else to go, I took a deep breath and turned down the corridor.

"Hello, Addie," he said as I neared.

"I have to get these suits to Coddles," I replied, trying to inch by.

"I think," he said, "you had better come in here first."

In my cubicle, the computer was entirely assembled and blinking obnoxiously at me. Jeff held out three inches of snipped red wire coated in nougat. I pretended to be shocked, but he held up a fat hand, stanching my performance. Then he motioned for me to follow him down the hallway to an unused company coat closet in the other wing. He called it his office and asked me to step inside. Then he closed the door behind us.

"Hello," I said, preparing for an onslaught of unnatural caresses.

But he switched on a low-watt bulb and began speaking in a quiet voice. "Yes, hello. This was a very interesting problem. Very interesting indeed. The reason for your computer malfunction appears to be related to this length of wire and a Zero candy bar—one of my favorites. It seems that someone opened up your hard drive and severed—"

I interrupted, pleading for mercy in a strained voice. If I were a spy, I would buckle instantly under any type of questioning!

But Fat Bald Jeff merely smiled and whispered, "I'm somewhat impressed."

This stopped me instantly.

"Oh, not at the amateurish, bungling sabotage," he went on, "but at your complete disregard for authority and your employer's property."

Haltingly, I replied, "Yes, well . . . down with the pig system and all that."

He sat on a box of old Christmas decorations, which groaned under his tonnage. "I had you pegged for a little brownnose yes-girl. But you seem to have a certain depth of depravity that I admire."

I sat opposite him on a stack of posters for the annual staff Hot Dog Day. "I do?"

He nodded. "You don't want to do your website project, do you?"

It all came tumbling out: my hatred of the job, of the new tasks that would go unpaid; the lurching zombies, the pathetic pep rallies masquerading as staff meetings, the lousy Christmas parties, the bank art, the recycled air, the windows that refused to open, the buzzing fluorescent lights, the beige walls, my God the beige walls!

"Are you going to turn me in?" I asked.

"I'm not interested in punishing the weak. I have bigger plans. I am interested, however, in what you might do for me." He leaned in expectantly.

I considered my options; what had *I* to offer? Then it struck me. I handed him the envelope with Coddles's nudie garbage, explaining its origin.

Fat Bald Jeff nodded seriously. A fractured smile curved his mouth as he slid the envelope into his shirt pocket. He said he would help me with the Web project if I would help him put a few ideas of his into motion. We struck a bargain. It was terribly exciting!

Day's end came quickly. I returned the dry cleaning to Coddles, who made me cough up the missing seventy-five cents I spent on lemonade. With a cursory glance at my bust, he sent me on my way. I had not really expected him to ask for the missing pornography but nevertheless felt relieved when I left the office.

Of course, I got stuck next to a lunatic on the stinking bus. He smelled like the biohazard Dumpster and I sent him many disapproving looks throughout the ride. It all goes back to diet, and finally I gently informed him that a preponderance of junk in the intestines can only cause discomfort to the body and to those around it.

He regarded me coldly, then stared straight ahead. Our society is in a shambles. Those of us with wisdom have a responsibility to share it with the unfortunates. But the unfortunates are always so damned ungrateful.

Walking back to my building, the stench of the lunatic still floated around me. His smell had attached itself to my clothes. Tonight I would have to do laundry. I shook my head sadly, yet with infinite patience for the world's idiots. I felt around in my bag for my keys, which must have gotten pushed to the bottom. The horrible smell doubled in intensity. I reached, grabbed hold of something, and pulled out—rancid tofurkey tarragon with havarti on millet bread!

Chapter

4

Val made us a delicious dinner. He rarely cooks in the middle of the week, and never for both of us, but he must have felt guilty for leaving me alone the past several nights while he and 2F gallivanted about town. He lingered by the doorway last evening as I scrubbed the baseboards inside the storage closet.

"I'm just running up to the grocery store with the guys," he said. "Need anything?"

I crawled out of the closet to respond, but he'd already left, shut the door, and locked it. Val's meaningless social conventions are so irritating. Anyway, tonight he made us a heavenly meal of poached sea bass with roasted red pepper sauce. He seemed appreciative of the culinary advice I offered, yet disregarded all my tips.

We used Grandmother's old Franciscan pattern china and Val's prized smoked-glass NFL tumblers from the gas station. Val always gets the Bears glass, while I drink out of the Browns or sometimes the Steelers. I feel a kinship with those industrial giants and would never use the namby-pamby Miami Dolphins glass, with its hideous colors and dangerously chipped rim. The NFL tumblers are, to me, another sure sign of spring. Each September, Val packs them away with his summer clothes in a footlocker. He says they have to be put away before the Bears' season starts, or he will end up breaking all the glasses in the set. During the winter we drink our vodka, milk, juice, and rum out of thrift-store ceramic mugs. I'm not fond of putting my mouth on strangers' drinking vessels, but I can't allow my collection of Fire King cups to be jeopardized by Val's drunken flailing. Why, last summer Val and I often drove his 1972 Buick Electra down Michigan Avenue at midnight, tipsy on Bull's Blood—a scandalous Hungarian red wine. He had his Bears tumbler in the car and stopped at each red light to swill the Bull's Blood and shout "Chicago: hog butcher to the world!" out the window. I realize now how hazardous that could have been: he might have dropped the glass outside the car, and we never would have been able to replace it. Well, thank God the Fire King is safely stored away in the hutch. I will probably bring it out at my and the Lemming's engagement party, provided the guests sign a waiver.

After dinner, we retired to the living room. I offered Val dibs on the disco couch, but he said he was going to work on a project with 2F. That's three nights this week he has abandoned me for *them*. I sniffed in response.

"Oh, for cryin' out Pete," he said. "We're just going to work in the yard. The landlord asked us to landscape a little and put in a garden. He's paying for it." I nearly seized up in shock, but Val missed my performance as he answered a knock at our door. *Val Wayne*, working with the earth! I don't believe it. The closest Val has ever come to communing with nature was a furtive romp under our dead evergreens with some anonymous tart last August.

He opened the door and there stood 2F, in all their snobby glory. In walked the Asian gentleman who had abused me for vacuuming the hall, followed by a sort of Teutonic masterpiece with the cheekbones of the impossibly well bred. Both wore pristine wheat overalls and rugged Eddie Bauer flannels and coats.

"You know Chung and Stefan," Val said. I bobbed my head like an imbecile and smiled stiffly.

"Your mustache looks absolutely lush," gushed Stefan.

"Yes," agreed Mr. Chung, "you look just like Billy Dee Williams." Val nodded with a sidelong glance at me. The smug bastard! I told him not even a month ago that he bore a striking resemblance to Lando Calrissian, but he just laughed and said flattery would not get him to hand over the last airplane bottle of Stoli. Hmph. I was simply trying to initiate a friendly conversation about stupid space fiction.

"Where are you going?" I asked in my smallest, least obtrusive, loneliest voice.

They exchanged fearful glances and told me they were going to Home Depot for some gardening tools and good dirt. It would be no fun, they lamented, I would certainly be bored there.

That's true. It's boring haggling with pimply teenage clerks over inferior shrubbery and complicated grout bags. I went into my room while the boys made a shopping list. Doesn't Val know that my horticultural knowledge could be put to use in our yard? Doesn't he care that old Gran has ripped away my usual summer garden project and I'm longing for fun times?

Made up my mind to stay in my room until Val begged for help, but I heard the boys quibbling over the benefits of grafting apple trees onto pear-tree root stock, so I tiptoed out. They'd already started down the stairs, however, and I didn't want to shout after them. Stinking 2F. It would be just like them to pervert the normal growth of tender saplings.

Threw myself on my bed in a fit, but tantrum-ing isn't much fun when you haven't an audience. Began to feel quite alone in the world (the sensitive usually are), so I relented in my grudge against the old woman and called her. Her phone rang and rang, and I was convinced she was outside spreading mulch with that horticultural carpetbagger next door. But finally, she answered on the fourteenth ring. Her voice sounded crackly and paper-thin. She scolded me for calling so late (eight-thirty) and said she had to get up early for a doctor's appointment.

"Gran! What's wrong? Should I come out there?" I asked in a panic. That trollop Fate was punishing me for my uncharitable thoughts about Grandmother!

"Cataracts," she said succinctly. "Nothing you can do. Doctor's going to see how long we can stave off the inevitable."

Dear, brave Grandmother. I offered to steal Jann's shabby station wagon, but she said my aunt Jane would drive her to the appointment. Aunt Jane is my father's elder sister and disapproves of Mother heartily, yet we don't get along. I don't know why. Her family benefited greatly from Father's desertion of the family pharmaceuticals firm, so she should be properly grateful that I am not out to reclaim my squandered inheritance.

Grandmother reminded me repeatedly not to bother Mother about the doctor's appointment or her generally deteriorating health or loneliness.

"Do you know, I wandered out into the kitchen one night last week to get myself a cup of warm milk, and the next thing I knew, I was facedown in the boxwood," she confided. "Don't worry your mother about it. It's just one of my spells."

Grandmother's spells seem to occur after her nightcaps of warm milk. I suspect the milk is sour.

With difficulty, I apologized to Gran for being mad at her about the garden. She said, "Pardon?" so often that I ended up saying I was sorry eighteen times before she understood me. Her hearing usually checks out when I need to apologize for something or thank her. The emotionally charged atmosphere wreaks havoc with her ancient ears.

After hanging up, I called Mother and told her all about Grandmother's eyes and decaying body. She muffled the receiver with her hand, but I distinctly heard voices and Scandinavian braying. I think it's disgraceful the way she neglects her dead husband's mother. It's one thing to abandon more distant relatives, but this one is her daughter's own Gran! You'd think that alone would endear the old lady to Mother, but it actually seems to repel her further.

"After all, Mother, I do have some of Grandmother's blood running through my veins," I said reproachfully.

She sighed. "Addie, I wouldn't be surprised if your veins run with vinegar."

I didn't know if she was implying that I'm an *alcoholic* or merely *vitriolic*, but I knew that I was insulted.

Turned out the light and tried to cry into my pillow, but it's awkward for me to weep when I can't see what I'm doing. I turned the light back on, which helped a little. Then I panicked because I remembered I had just restuffed my pillow with buckwheat hulls and didn't know if salt water would harm them. A girl can't have decent histrionics when constantly beset with domestic worries.

Heard the pitiful, desperate whining of a dog outside. Looked out my bedroom window and saw a small white pup in a cage on the fire escape of the building next door. Felt sad for him. Here we were, two creatures abandoned by humanity, left to cry alone in the night. I opened the window a crack so that I could utter a few soothing words to him across the gangway, just like prisoners of war sequestered in different stalags. But before I could think of something appropriate to say, a man stomped out onto the fire escape and dumped a bucket of water on top of the dog and yelled at it to shut up. I jumped back into bed, threw the down comforter over my head, and trembled a bit. What kind of a society are we living in?

Another workshop with the Jeffs. As promised, Fat Bald Jeff did my sample assignment at his computer and e-mailed it to me. I wonder what I will have to do for him in return? We never quite discussed what part I would play in his plans, or what he meant by "putting his ideas into motion." Some kind of menial task, I expect, like petitioning the management to serve cocktail weenies at the Christmas party instead of stale crullers. I forwarded the sample Web assignment on to Coddles as though I had worked on it myself. I am getting better at this technology. I feel sorry for people who are too stupid to use the computer. It can simplify one's life so much.

Elevator was sick again, so I had to trudge up the stairs with Bev and Francis after the workshop. Francis patiently waited for me to catch up at the landings while Bev bellowed heartlessly about how the thin don't live as long as the robust. That's because the robust usually squash us when no one else is looking, but I was too out of breath to say anything.

Went into the staff lounge in our wing and got my lunch out of the refrigerator. I suppose from now on I will always feel a dreadful anxiety as I open the fridge door. My subconscious will never forget the awful day my sandwich disappeared. To think some deranged personality stole my lunch out of the fridge, then snuck it back into my purse, all without my knowing. Now I find myself looking at my coworkers with suspicion. How sad that I've lost my childlike trust of humankind.

Eating quarters in the lounge are dusty and surrounded on three sides by shelves of books we have published on library cataloging rules. I am usually the only one who eats there, but the solitude aids my digestion. Most zombies eat in the dungeon and the rest eat at restaurants or in their cubicles. Mr. Genett tried to establish a new law prohibiting employees from eating in their cubicles, but the whole publishing staff rioted in response. It all goes back to peons thinking of their cubes as home. Don't they know better? My rule: no food and no decor in my cubicle; although today I taped to my wall a diagram of a hunchback sitting at a computer terminal, which I hope will remind me to sit up straight.

I was cutting my peanut butter sandwich into aesthetically pleasing strips, instead of one gargantuan hod, when the graphic designers trooped in. Francis smiled, but the other two ignored me.

"Can you believe that flyer by the 'vator, man?" asked one.

"That old chick with her boob in the martini glass! Sick," agreed the other.

I cut my sandwich strips into minuscule pieces.

Francis tried to involve me in their discussion, but I concentrated on my cutlery. He said, "I heard there were flyers up by the elevator on each floor, but the unit heads ran around like mad tearing them down. Did you see them, Addie?"

"I didn't do anything. I don't know what you're talking about," I said as my forehead became clammy and moist. I blotted my face with a soiled paper napkin. *This* is what it's like holding up under rabid inquisition. Perhaps I could be a spy. No one's getting anything out of me. Calm, calm. Ah, yes . . . my face was a cool, impenetrable mask.

Francis said, "You got some peanut butter in your eyebrows."

Wiped off peanut butter with lunch bag. Mask still held up, though fissures tried to crack through. "Er . . . yes, well," I said.

The other two designers exited the lounge with their sack lunches, imitating me and mincing about. Expertly, I changed the subject.

"They're not very nice."

"Those flyers? Yeah, I guess—"

"No, no," I said, "the other graphic delinquents."

He frowned. "Graphic *designers.*"

I said nothing. Francis's untamed black brows deepened his frown. "So, did you see the picture?"

I scrunched up my eyes and nose, the way people do when they're struggling to dredge up some buried memory.

"Did I see the flyers? No, of course not! Ha-ha! I don't know what you mean. What flyers? I didn't put them up, nobody saw me, you can't prove anything. Ha-ha! Er . . ." Again with the moist salty stuff running down my face. My throat was parched, as from a powerful sirocco zipping through the Gobi. I glugged the rest of my water. My breath came shallow, swift. Lying does not come easy to sensitive people with acute digestive disorders.

Francis laughed. "Next you'll be telling me it was your husband's idea to murder King Duncan and that you had nothing to do with it."

"What?" I cried. My house of lies had come tumbling down around me like faulty Tinker Toys.

He said, "From *Macbeth*? Ah, never mind . . ."

I laid my head down on the table, pretending a migraine. Curse that Fat Bald Jeff for enticing me into a web of deceit. Putting up the copies of that yucko picture of Coddles's seemed like fun at the time, but now that I know what it is to be mired in deception and crime, I will surely pay with nervous insomnia and irritable bowel syndrome the rest of my days.

Francis, oblivious to my discomfort, went on about the flyer. He said its caption announced that the original photo had been found in the dungeon microwave and could be claimed at the front desk.

"Isn't that a riot? I wonder who did it?" he asked.

Just at the point of my confessing to it all, Bev walked into the lounge. Seizing the opportunity, I indicated her to Francis by wild eyebrow activity. Why not blame it on her, horrible bloated sheep that she is? Lura followed after, and they all had a lengthy discussion about the flyers as I chewed off my hangnails.

"I think it's just disgusting," said Bev. She angrily jabbed the buttons on the pop machine and it spat a Mello Yello at her.

"Methinks the sheep doth protest too much," I squeaked in a voice two octaves higher than usual. Unfortunately, this comment directed all attention to me. I felt a confession coming on, as I cannot hold up under public scrutiny, but used my last bit of control to rise from my chair to leave.

Francis looked disappointed; I'm sure he was planning to grill me some more. Lura grabbed my vacated chair and Bev lumbered off down the corridor with her oily beverage and bucket of fried bird.

Back in the cube I sat down at the computer. Saw that Coddles had sent a global e-mail to all staff in the building. It read:

> Someone sent a rude letter to the CTA from this office
> and signed my name. I warn you, this is a punishable
> offense, sending business letters on company sta-
> tionery and signing others' names.

I heard yelling in the hallway, and I gophered over my cubicle wall to see what was going on. Mr. Genett was scolding Coddles for using the e-mail system to air his personal grievances! Coddles insisted he had every right to do so, since one of the employees used the National Association of Libraries' stationery, signed his name, and sent it from our building. Mr. Genett just shook his head, saying that's not what e-mail is for. I have to agree with Mr. Genett.

Unfortunately, I was standing on my folding chair and happened to look down at Bev in her cubicle, sucking the marrow out of the stripped chicken bones. Immediately overcome with nausea, I fell off the chair and hit my head on the cubicle wall, which wobbled a bit but remained rooted. Coddles and Mr. Genett rushed to my aid before I could properly arrange myself, and I fear they got an eyeful of ripped gray underpants. I'm not proud of the state of my undergarments, but there it is.

I thought I heard Coddles grunt, "Oh mama," as he took in the sight at his feet. His strand of hair came unglued from his head and trembled spasmodically between his blackcurrant eyes. He helped me into my folding chair and asked, between heavy moist breaths, if I was all right. Why couldn't suave Genett be the one helping and patting and cooing over me? *He* just looked me over to ensure no lawsuit would be forthcoming, then hastened back to the executive wing. Coddles fussed over me while a line of drool swung from his fish lips.

Felt my nostrils flare involuntarily while my mouth widened into a stricken line of poorly masked horror. My eyes began to tear as the stench of brine and brilliantine soaked the air around me. I shouted, "I'm all *right*," which at least compelled him to release his grip on my shoulders.

He sat down in my extra folding chair and dabbed at his forehead with the paper in his hand. I stared at this strange method of mopping up perspiration. He looked at his hand and threw the paper down pettishly. As he fished through the voluminous folds of his *prêt-à-porter* suit for a hanky, I easily read a paragraph from the paper on the floor. It was from the CTA.

. . . very sorry indeed about your sexual episode and sick grandmother! Try as we might to enforce behavior codes on the trains, it is not always possible. Neither is it practical to station armed guards in each car to beat off unwanted advances! Lives at stake and all that! Please accept our apologies and keep riding the El! Chicago, the city that works!

> Sincerely,
> Ian el-Sabbah

No doubt some CTA flunky. Coddles saw me reading the letter but didn't seem to care. I suspect he has other troubles on his mind—such as how someone got ahold of his porno picture and Xeroxed it all over the building! He stuffed the letter in his coat pocket and expectorated into his vile rough-edged hanky. Frankly, his handkerchief makes my proletarian underpants look like silk organza.

He stood up to leave, blubbering into the cloth, "Stupid letter. I don't understand why he used so many exclamation points."

I didn't know either but replied that the exclamation point is a grammatical crutch used by overexpressive underachievers, which seemed to comfort him a little.

That Ian el-Sabbah seems like a self-righteous little prig. I predict more letters will be flooding his in box over the next few weeks.

After that haunting episode, I decided to settle my nerves with a sweet treat from the vending machine in the dungeon. I saw Fat Bald Jeff standing in front of the machine, as was his thrice-a-day custom, pouring in vast amounts of change and draining its stock of Bun, a strange and arcane clod of candy. He stuffed his pants pockets full of Buns, a sight I cannot adequately describe. I wanted to say: *I'm done with our life of crime! I'm being crushed by the burden of our hoax!* But as he passed by, he winked at me. It was a sign of solidarity. I realized I'd had a partner in something, however brief, for the first time in my life. Winked back.

At the vending machine, I suddenly wondered if in fact he *had* winked, or was it just a coincidental spasm? *My* wink truly conveyed brotherhood in a secret society. *His* just looked like the lazy-eyed twitch of a psychotic pirate. Oh well.

Dropped my quarters in and chose the Zero candy bar. The white chocolate cramps my ascending colon, but after my debut into lawless society, the pawing of Coddles, and the display of my grundies, I no longer care.

After days of begging, I finally convinced Mother that we ought to go see Grandmother. She stopped by my building one evening to pick me up. As I feared, she brought the lumbering Swede along. Instead of exiting the car and ringing my buzzer like a civilized person, Jann merely sat in the driver's seat and laid on the horn. Paco and the giantess sat on the front stoop, sharing a butt, and glared reproachfully at the oaf behind the wheel. I was embarrassed for Paco to watch me get in that honking hunk of junk with those two morons, but I could see no way out of it.

Sat in the backseat and congratulated Jann on his Scandinavian doorbell. My dry humor flies right over the philistine's head. He peeled out, with the diesel station wagon spewing black fog, and drove like a madman up the Kennedy Expressway.

Mother said that my grandmother tends to exaggerate her illnesses and that we were probably taking a trip out to Evanston for nothing. She said Jann's mother is almost ninety, still cuts her own firewood with a handsaw, and never complains about her health or anything else. I pointed out that Jann's mother enjoys good health because, like a captive whale, she subsists on a diet entirely of herring, and the reason she has nothing to complain about, unlike Gran, is that she does not have my mother for a daughter-in-law.

"Not yet," said Mother.

Felt queasy the rest of the ride.

Gran's daffodils were in bloom in front of the house. I reminded Mother of the autumn we helped Gran plant a hundred daffodils and two hundred tulips, and the picnic lunch we ate outside afterward. Mother said all she remembered was that the squirrels dug up every tulip bulb by the next morning and that Grandfather went out with his .22 and shot them in the trees. He received a stern lecture from the police but was not arrested. He'd donated a lot of money to the city of Evanston in one form or another and in those days was considered an eccentric. Mother said he was lucky he was rich, otherwise he would have been merely criminal.

Grandmother was playing solitaire in her parlor. She had the heat turned up to eighty and wore a beige cardigan, even though I've told her thousands of times that beige makes her look bilious. At least she had on lipstick, a good indication that she was feeling all right. I sat next to her on the raspberry divan and kissed her on the cheek while Mother made a poor show of concern, fluffing pillows vaguely and turning the thermostat down. Jann stood rigidly in the corner, fiddling with the drawstring of his extremely tight sport pants.

Mother began, "So how are—"

Grandmother lifted her hand for quiet, saying, "Hold on, dear. This solitaire is going to come out. Red six on black seven. Move the king. Ah, yes."

Mother rolled her eyes to the heavens, sighed, and sat in the Queen Anne chair, looking horribly incongruous with her flared overalls and wraithlike gray hair. She leaned in toward Gran and shouted, "Old woman. *Old woman.* What did the doctor say?"

I am proud Gran had the poise to ignore Mother's insults. She finished her play of cards, then muttered, "Drat. Two of clubs."

Jann took a step out of the corner and said, "You're only supposed to look at every third card." A frosty silence descended upon the parlor, and Jann retreated into his corner.

Grandmother pulled a pink shawl around her shoulders. "Chilly in here. Ruth, turn that thermostat up. The doctor says the eyes are deteriorating, but I'm in no immediate danger."

Relieved, I snuggled up to her and she put her arm around me.

Mother stood and rubbed her hands together. "Marvelous. Well, shall we get going?"

My poison darts found their mark and Mother sank into the chair. Gran put down her cards on the end table (Jacobean—yuck, a flea-market gift from Father) and gazed up lovingly at the framed portraits on the wall above.

"Here we go," muttered Mother.

Gran sighed and straightened a photograph of Father at age twenty. His hair was combed and clean, unlike the horrible corona of brambles that I remembered, and he wore a tie and smiled for the camera. The picture was taken when Grandfather still expected his son to follow him into the family pharmaceuticals firm. A good decade later Father finally saw the error of his ways and decided to go to work at the firm, but by then our family unit was on the verge of collapse.

"Such a handsome boy, Harvey was," she said, "so much potential. And we thought that houndstooth sack suit was so *outrageous* then! If we'd only known what hideous costumes men would wear today." Her voice trailed off and we all looked at Jann's purple and orange tiger-striped Zubaz exercise pants. He tried to cross his legs casually, but his thighs were too massive.

Gran looked at Mother and beamed. "He *was* handsome, wasn't he?"

Glumly, Mother nodded.

"Thin, bookish, intellectual. Not like . . . er, young fellow there." Gran can hardly bring herself to pronounce the bricklayer's absurd Scandinavian name without going apoplectic.

We all heard Jann's stomach gurgle from across the room.

"Oh my," said Grandmother, rising from the divan, "I suppose it's dinnertime. I was just going to have some cottage cheese and fruit, but you take it, young man."

Jann, unaccustomed to Grandmother's circular etiquette, practically ran into the kitchen. Mother followed him while I coaxed Gran to sit back down. She picked up her cards again and peeked under the two of clubs. Then she asked me about Martin. It's so difficult to talk about him because, on the one hand, I would like to move this courtship on to the next level—selecting the Waterford "Marquis" pattern for our stemware—but on the other hand, he's a tedious pedant who doesn't seem to view me as a potential mate. Once I brought him here for dinner. Grandmother asked several times about his intentions, but he just remarked endlessly on the prudence of capital investment.

Grandmother had smiled brightly and said, "I'm sure that's very nice, dear, but don't you want someone to share it with?" as she offered him a third helping of boiled broccoli.

He said, "Good God, no."

Their eyes met and I sensed an unspoken challenge. She said, "But broccoli's so good for the skin," with a pitying glance at his acne scars. I had been gulping Strawberry Hill by the glassful, and luckily, I gagged at just the right moment during their confused exchange. Gran walloped me something fierce on the back while the Lemming brooded with his fingertips stuck in his pockmarks.

"Martin's fine," I said.

"Wedding bells yet?" she asked. I flung myself facedown on the sofa in response.

She patted my head consolingly as I wept of my failure to land him. Without the Lemming, I am bereft of prospects. All I want is a house and a garden and a manservant named Tressilian imported from the Cornish coast.

I heard Mother approach from the kitchen. Jann trailed after her, whining, "Can't you get her to make something with a little meat in it?" I sat up and dried my eyes before Mother could see that I'd been crying. Nothing is worse than my mother's attempts at comfort. She has the maternal aptitude of a serving fork.

"All ready?" she asked. I nodded, got up, and kissed Gran on the cheek.

Mother narrowed her eyes suspiciously at me. She asked if Grandmother had been dosing me with homemade cherry brandy again. Grandmother sniffed and walked stiffly up the stairs without a word.

If my parents hadn't determined to ruin our lives and squander my inheritance on the vile VW minibus, things might have been different for me. But Fate has always been a sorry jade when I try to count on her. Even though Father refused to support us until I was nine, it's possible we *could* have turned out normal. He did eventually submit to Grandfather's plea to shut down the sickening kiln and take up work at the pharmaceuticals firm. For four years, we were nearly solvent. Father dragged himself out of the house every morning to sell products, and Mother stopped fashioning plant holders and vests out of hemp. She even cooked a sort of evening meal for us, but it was usually wrecked by the addition of kelp and gritty leaves.

Father suffered, going to the salt mines each morning. He missed lying in bed till noon and firing misshapen clay pots. He came home from work in the evening, replaced his tie and slacks with a traumatic sort of feminine caftan, and shuffled around our hut, murmuring, "Another day closer to death." Then Mother would stare out the kitchen window at our rusting Volvo and say, sighing, "Why was I born a woman? To bear the burden of some man's torment all my life?" Then she'd start bossing us around. Father had to wash the vegetables for dinner, and I had to scrub the bathtub so they could battle in the kitchen. I told my grandparents about the constant lack of civility in our house, and Grandfather said, "It's always the children who end up hurt when mothers neglect their duties. It's a wonder Addie turned out even half normal." Grandmother nodded and clucked her tongue. I lowered my eyes and looked sad.

Father ended up becoming so tiresome about his job that Mother locked herself in her sewing room and refused to clean or feed us! Father was like an infant in diapers, he was so helpless without her.

"How do you work this can opener?" he once asked me. I pointed out he didn't need a can opener for bottled beer, but he just got mad and heaved the thing against the wall. I cleaned up the mess while Father stalked around the house, screaming, "You have to come out of there sometime, Ruth! The child is starving."

She shouted back, "The cookbook's by the microwave." We had carrots and bread heels for dinner.

The final injustice came one morning as I dressed for school. My uniform skirt was stiff with grime between the pleats, so I brought it to Mother's attention. She was in the sewing room, stringing beads like a mental patient.

"My uniform's filthy," I said, "and the bus will be here in twenty minutes."

She examined the skirt abstractedly, then tossed it at me. "You could do with some earthiness, Miss Priss." It would serve her right to have Child Welfare spot me on the way to school, disheveled as an orphan. I was willing to withstand the cruel inattention of a foster home if it would teach my parents something about responsibility. I mentioned as much to Mother and she said, "How quick can you pack your bags?" Callous birth-giver! She's always had a streak of selfishness that stuns me.

Well, one day Father finally got Mother to come out of isolation. She was making a macramé owl to hang in the sewing room, and I was cleaning our disgrace of a kitchen. We both heard a manic honking in the driveway and wandered outside to see what was wrong. There sat Father, grinning madly, in a Volkswagen minibus painted a lurid shade of mustard. Mother squealed and ran toward the heap. I cast about furtively, hoping the neighbors were not witnessing our domestic drama. Father had quit his job at the pharmaceuticals firm and was taking us on the road to live as vagabonds!

He planned to support us by selling homeopathic remedies on our travels. I looked to Mother for help, but she agreed with him that living far from a capitalist hive would do us all some good. I even appealed to my grandparents, but they tearfully shook their heads.

"Can nothing be done?" I demanded, outraged. "I can't live in a bus with those people."

Grandmother sniffed. "She may have no maternal feeling, but she's still your mother."

Against my will, I packed my belongings: pink party dress, twenty pairs of white underpants, drudge garments that Mother threw in, dish towels, two cans of Bon Ami, toothbrush, travel journal with lock, hairbrush, sponge curlers, and a bottle of 409. I also packed Windex to clean the dust of endless flatlands off the bus windows, but Mother took it out of my bag and showed it to Father, who collapsed in hysterics. Father then made some tasteless remarks about one day getting a paternity test! I expected Mother to fume at this blasphemy, but she just giggled. I found his comments about my parentage offensive in the extreme. I don't like to speak ill of the dead, but my father was an idiot.

Walked in the door to find Val sucking away on limes and perusing my gardening books! Had I not suffered enough with the workload at the Place, my cubicle-induced head injury and subsequent exhibition of underpants, the terrible fondling of Coddles, the sandwich ordeal, the crying dog on the fire escape, my decrepit Gran, my loose-moraled mother, and King Sweno's road rage on the Kennedy? No. I had not suffered enough until all new gardening projects were denied me. The weak link to my sanity snapped. I strode up to the disco couch, fists clenched and eyes afire, my adorable chin-length bob swinging in rage. I was suddenly reminded of Gran's favorite biblical quote: "Tonight thy very soul will be required of thee." But I discarded it.

I wrenched the horrible lime rind from Val Wayne's mouth and flung it against the wall. He screamed—a tormented, agonized cry—and cursed me full in the face. In my fury I had torn off part of his mustache!

"Oh Val," I wailed, but he would have none of my sorrow. He ran into the bathroom and slammed the door, ignoring my pleas. I slumped outside the bathroom door in the hallway, trying to explain. The pathos of the situation revealed itself to me as I sat on the floor begging forgiveness in the midst of dust bunnies collecting at the edge of the baseboards. Only a pathetic creature as I would remain prostrate on such a smutty floor. But dust bunnies give me the heebie-jeebies, so I swept them aside with the broom and continued to cry from the comfortable disco couch. I could still be a sorrowful wretch without lying on the floor.

After thirty minutes I gave up. I got the ironing board out of the pantry, and immediately a calm suffused my body. Something about ironing is so steadying. I selected black cigarette pants and a red silk blouse with mandarin collar for tomorrow's wardrobe. I was taking no more chances and decided against wearing skirts to the Place for a while. Human nature being what it is, I'm afraid I'm unable to quit gophering over my cubicle walls. It's not my fault. If the walls went to the ceiling like they're supposed to, I would not be able to eavesdrop. I have nothing; why deny myself this one guilty pleasure? Studied my wardrobe choice for a few minutes. Decided I'm partial to the glamorous oriental look. My accoutrements were appropriate to the outfit, both in style (dragonfly barrette and fake jade bangle) and in origin (made in Taiwan).

Chose Chanel-ripoff black ballet flats and set them outside my closet, with bunion pads resting neatly on top. I will not sacrifice my feet to fashion and end up spending each Saturday morning for the next forty years at a sadistic Greek podiatrist's office. I hung the outfit on my closet doors in readiness. It was a smart, seductive look, particularly with my Godzilla-era Japanese scientist spectacles. Austin Powers, indeed!

I had just prepared a nightcap of warm milk and whiskey when the bathroom door opened. Val's eyes were puffy and red. He stumbled to the disco couch and collapsed. His upper lip looked absolutely wrecked. It appeared that he had been applying various salves and ointments to promote new hair growth and soothe the sting. But how can you soothe the sting of a decade's worth of hair farming lost in an instant?

I peeked timidly around the corner. I offered Val a hank of my hair to rip out, but he just made little sniffly sounds and stroked his ravaged lip. I offered him my milk and whiskey, which he grudgingly accepted. Then I threw myself upon his mercy and his lap.

"Forgive me!" I cried. "I didn't mean it!" In a torrent, I bawled about the garden and my disappointment at being left out.

"We weren't leaving you out. The garden is for everyone in the building. I just didn't think you wanted to tear up sod and rototill dead squirrels and syringes out of the ground."

I tried to administer comfort by murmuring softly and patting the little ruined hair patch, but he flung my hand away in anguish, hissing, "*Don't* touch it!" Then he stormed into his room and slammed the door so hard our brandy bottles rattled.

Went to bed. Deep Purple churned away at full volume from Val's room for eight straight hours.

Chapter 5

Val still isn't speaking to me. When he gets home from work, he changes his clothes, grabs a lime and the bottle of Bacardi, and heads down to 2F. The Bacardi is actually mine (a Christmas gift from Mother and Jann), but I dare not say a thing. This has left my evenings empty of human companionship and has forced me to seek solace in the paws of the Lemming. He's still stingy, but the more groping I allow, the better entertainment he provides. I would not like to announce what I endured to get a dinner at the Pump Room and a musical at the Shubert. It *cannot* be long before the blue box from Tiffany's makes its appearance!

I needed, however, a reprieve from his advances, so it was with anticipation that I looked forward to the invitation issued via e-mail from Fat Bald Jeff today.

> Dear friends:
> Please come over tonight for my birthday party, two doors down from the Chicken George on Huron St. near Damen Ave. This is my 36th, and coincidentally the 10th year I have worked for NAL tech support without a promotion or raise. There'll be cake and beer.
>
> Sincerely,
> Fat Bald Jeff

Since Fat Bald Jeff and I had embarked on the Porno Project at the copy machine the other week, we had grown a little closer, and I was pleased to be invited to his party. Didn't feel quite as nervous about our hoax anymore . . . after all, no one had caught us. Francis had quit grilling me. Jeff hinted about the "other plans" he wished us to undertake—and they are *much* more thrilling than begging the executives for Christmas cocktail weenies! He's still a tad secretive about what I am to do, exactly, but it involves some type of anonymous muckraking. Everyone knows I detest gossip and snooping and unkindness, of course, but I'm intrigued.

To ensure my participation in his future projects, Jeff has tackled my Web assignments with gusto, freeing up a lot of time for me to stare out the cubicle window. I asked him how he could possibly have time to do my assignments while working on his normal duties, but he just gave the Hole a bewildered look and said that apart from the occasional mechanical crisis, tech support had nothing to do.

At 12:05, Francis walked into the staff lounge. I was just about to take a bite of my tuna sandwich strip. I stopped and looked at him expectantly.

"Please don't stop on my account," he implored. "Go on, it's almost twelve-oh-six. I just wanted to know if you were going to Fat Bald Jeff's tonight."

I nodded and bit into the sandwich. He suggested we run out to Marshall Field's to buy Jeff a birthday present before our lunch hour was up. I replied that I had sneaked out of the building the instant I received his missive that morning and already purchased a gift.

Francis looked so dejected as he slumped into the chair across from me. Why not ask Lura, I offered. He hemmed and hawed. Thankfully, I was spared his further indecision by Lura herself as she walked toward the pop machine.

"Lura!" I called. "Francis here is looking for someone to help him select a present for Fat Bald Jeff's birthday." She agreed to accompany him.

He stood up, sighed, and muttered, "Thanks." He could at least *try* to appear grateful! I know he must have a secret crush on her, given her savage hair and wild undulating curves. I have a keen sense of such feelings in others.

Dashed off a quick note to the CTA.

Dear Ian el-Sabbah—if that is indeed your name:
Re: my letter of March 16
I am shocked and saddened by your unfeeling response to my plight on your train. Perhaps if *you* had been abused by a vulgar, deranged passenger, you would be quicker to react with some sympathy and action. As it is, I see I have no choice but to discontinue my use of the Red Line. That is, unless you attempt to exercise some standards when soliciting customers. And I found your careless reference to my grandmother in the same sentence as the words "sexual episode" profoundly offensive.

> No need to respond,
> Coddles

I was careful not to use any exclamation points. Difficult, as I was extremely emotionally charged.

When I arrived home, I found Val and 2F poring over hair-style catalogs. Stefan had been a struggling hairdresser when Mr. Chung came along and saved him from a life of cosmetic servitude. He still had his old hairstyle manuals, I suppose, to keep his hand in. Just like I plan to keep *The Chicago Manual of Style,* fourteenth edition, after Martin whisks me away, even though I will have no further need for grammatical precision, barring the occasional letter to Grandmother.

Three sets of eyes regarded me icily as I meekly hung up the false Burberry. If only I had been wearing my mandarin-collar blouse that day! Chung might have been more disposed to kindness. As it was, I tiptoed past the glacier into the kitchen and made myself a simple meal of canned peas, toast, and champagne. I made a big show of popping the cork and squealing, "Ooh! Bubbly," when it hit the ceiling, so that 2F would realize that I was the type of person who always had a bottle of champagne lying around. It was likely that Fat Bald Jeff would have some food at his party, but heaven knows I can't stomach offal. I ate at our little wooden table and looked out the window at our backyard. From the third floor it was hard to see what progress they had made in creating a garden, other than clearing out some rubble and trampling the one healthy patch of grass. No one came in to watch me drink champagne.

Why should I be exiled from my own living room? Val would have to come around sooner or later. I changed into a lovely silk kimono I got for three dollars at the thrift and shuffled into the living room in a way that made my feet look tiny. I'd never had occasion to wear it before, but now that Mr. Chung was here, I'd have an appreciative admirer.

"Val, I know it's not as luxuriant as what you once had," said Stefan, with a pointed look in my direction, "but I think you should go for this one on page twelve. Fullness in the center, severely tapering off at the ends. Like David Niven."

"No, no," retorted Chung. "Niven's all wrong for him. He needs even coverage across the lip. Think Robert Redford in 1974."

This went on for a while. Poor Val thumbed listlessly through the book, stroking his bare patch. I thought he should have just shaved the whole thing off and begun again, but he'd probably be well into his forties before he got some decent results. Now he was stuck with adapting his half 'stache into a presentable style. Unfortunately, every time 2F showed him a possible selection, he just looked longingly at the Allman Brothers LP on his lap.

"This is what I've been shooting for," he said unhappily, showing them Duane Allman's stringy blond vermicelli. The boys sighed, frustrated with the stalemate.

"*I* know!" I shouted excitedly. "How about the mustache on the little balding man from *Magnum P.I.*?"

They looked at me as though I had suggested a Salvador Dalí or a Hercule Poirot.

Chung said, "If he's going to have anyone's mustache from *Magnum P.I.*, it's going to be Tom Selleck's, not the little balding guy's."

"I *hate* the little balding guy's mustache!" said Val. "Besides, he looks like Hitler. That's great, Addie. You want a black man to wear a Hitler mustache. Great idea."

"It's not like Hitler," I squeaked, alarmed at the erupting chaos. "It's like . . . like David Niven more than Hitler."

Stefan rolled his eyes to the ceiling. "It's *nothing* like Niven."

I stood up. A single tear slid down my cheek, and I cinched my kimono tightly. We sensitive persons can't take public outrage. I whimpered a little as I shuffled out of the living room. Perhaps the pathetic figure I drew softened Val's flinty heart.

"Wait. Where are you going?" he asked.

I blew my nose in my embroidered handkerchief after first flourishing it in front of 2F. Just because I am friendless and alone in the world and have accidentally ruined Val's mustache, it doesn't mean I can't appreciate quality linens. I explained to Val about Fat Bald Jeff's party.

He stared at my kimono. "Is that what you're wearing?"

"Oh no, it's just a robe. This might interest you," I said to Chung, confidence surging as I twirled and modeled my kimono. "It's from China."

"This might interest *you*," he replied. "I'm from Michigan."

I fled into my closet. Curse the inscrutable Oriental!

I pulled my nine-hundred-pound bike out of the storage room in the basement, clamped on my driving goggles over my spectacles, secured the trusty rain bonnet, and set off toward Jeff's. I didn't mind an occasional burst of exercise, especially as Jeff didn't live far and I was too afraid to ask Val to lend me bus fare. Anyway, the bus route that goes by Jeff's house is unspeakable. Much wiser to avoid it altogether. Unfortunately, riding the bike means wearing trousers. I've never been to a party wearing trousers before. I hope the other guests will understand.

Wrapped Jeff's gift in company stationery during the afternoon. It got tossed around in my plastic handlebar basket during the ride, but I think it will be okay. I selected for his present a small spiral-bound journal in which to compose his thoughts. Frankly, I doubt Jeff has many thoughts that are not of a rambling, paranoid nature, but I can't help what he writes in there.

As I neared the address I became more and more dismayed. Jeff lives in a shantytown! The houses were all dilapidated and festooned with plastic Santas. Groups of menacing young toughs stood about idly on corners. One of them called out, "Hey mama" as I pedaled by. Why is it men feel compelled to cry out for their mamas when I am around? There is nothing in the least maternal about me. In fact, there is probably no one in the world less motherly than I—except, of course, my mother.

I would not be surprised if a gang of thugs, attracted by the present in my basket, ambushed me and ran off with Jeff's gift. I shuddered to imagine some hooligan writing earnestly each night in the purloined journal. Just like Dostoyevsky's postal worker.

Finally reached Jeff's address. The number was scrawled on fake brick siding with a Sharpie. In his front yard—a rubbish-strewn square of filth and weeds—stood a grotesque semblance of a mongrel dog. It looked at me with baleful eyes, which ran freely with a yellowish substance. It was tied up by a chain massive enough to restrain an elephant. The fur stood out in patches from its misshapen body, and scabbish, pink skin made up the rest. Even its tail, a bloodied stub that crooked out from its rump, looked diseased. I opened the front gate and timidly crept in, and the dog became a snapping, salivating mass of mange and gore. It strained at the end of its chain—mere inches away! Couldn't tell if the chain would extend to the sidewalk at the point I would have to cross the dog, so I stood uncertainly by the gate, shielding myself with the massive bike. Was appalled at the plastic garden gnome standing sentry by a dead rhododendron.

Moments later, Fat Bald Jeff hurried out from the rear of the building. He waved me in, saying the dog would not be able to reach me. I inched my way down the walk, pressed between the chain-link fence on my right and the iron bicycle on my left. Felt brave.

"Sorry about that," said Jeff as I reached him. "It doesn't like me either. Want to lock up your bike down here? I live on the third floor." He indicated our route: a hundred-year-old wooden fire escape painted a hideous shade of battleship gray.

· I gulped. "I'll carry it up." I had a lock, but I was not about to have one of those street thugs try to wrest away my only vehicle.

I got up two steps and fell down. Jeff had to come back and hoist the bike on my shoulder so that I could try again. Made it all the way up on the sixth try. Set the bike down on the small landing in front of his door, gaining my breath. It was thoughtful of Jeff to wait for me to get up there.

"There's a kind of moistness on my neck and face," I said. I touched the skin gingerly. Clammy.

"Well . . . I think it's sweat," he replied.

"What do you mean?"

"Sweat. You know, from physical exertion." He looked at me as if I were an idiot.

Ugh. There was soreness now, too, in my arms. I must be coming down with the flu. Sweat! Please. Sweating is for oxen and terrariums.

We walked in. Jeff hung up my rain bonnet and driving goggles on a crude Peg-Board by the door. I wheeled my bike over to a load-bearing beam in the middle of the loft and locked it. I recognized some Hole denizen watching me nearby, stuffing its face with chocolate-covered pretzels. He asked if I thought someone there was going to steal my bike. I think my meaningful gaze answered his question.

Jeff lives not only in a shantytown, but in a shanty! When he said he lived on the third floor, he meant the attic of the house. The pitched roof prohibited any upright movement save in the direct center of the loft. Those taller than five foot seven had to crouch. Luckily, Jeff is quite short and walks around hunched over like a simian anyway. No walls to be seen. His kitchen consisted of a hotplate plugged into a gigantic power strip by his bed. I counted eight plugs attached to the surge protector—its own cord was attached to a series of extension cords that trailed across the room and out the back window.

I counted among the guests Bev, Lura, and seventeen men. Ordinarily this ratio would please me, except tonight the men were all zombies from the Place. Many had not even changed out of their work clothes! Earl the unarmed desk official was there, still in his dull uniform with dubious SECURITY patch. In the corner, scraping the crab-dip bowl with his fingers, stood Other Jeff. It was a good thing that years of poor posture at the computer terminal had permanently bowed his back, as he never would have been able to stand up straight in this loft. He picked a thick, coiled hair out of the dip and wiped it on the back of his pants.

I made small talk with him about the dangers of decaying foam-rubber baseball caps as he cast about the room in a forlorn manner. He must have been searching out more crab dip. He began to wander away bit by bit, looking for the dip, but I kept pace with him. Suddenly he broke into a run—quite an unusual sight, as he was bent over like a shepherd's crook—and ran smack into Francis. I was momentarily impeded by a gyrating zombie (someone had thrown a record on the hi-fi), and it took me a second to disentangle myself from the mess. I heard Other Jeff beg Francis for help, since some girl was following him around. What girl? I hadn't seen anyone following us. Then I turned and saw Lura a few feet away, filling a cup at the keg. Can't imagine why she would follow around Other Jeff. Poor darling must be terribly lonely.

"Care to dance?" Francis surprised me, stealing up that way. He smiled in a way that must charm other women and held out his arm. The music grew louder and shook the attic walls. Techies fought over the hi-fi: the young geeks insisted on the Chemical Brothers; old ones preferred Jethro Tull and Foghat. How does one dance to Foghat? I took Francis's arm, and he led me into a disgusting group of prancing hobbits.

I am a lovely dancer. I know this because Grandmother told me so when I was a teen. We used to trade Grandfather off on each other during our scandalous three-way fox-trots. I can also frug with the best of them, but I am not familiar with today's moronic hoof jigging. Francis flopped around, apparently stricken with Saint Vitus's Dance, as I gaped openly in horror. Even Fat Bald Jeff flailed around the room, bouncing like a depraved and wrathful beach ball. Tried to mimic Francis's palsy but felt that unpleasantly moist, sticky sensation on the back of my neck again.

"Sorry," I screamed over the Foghat, "I don't feel well."

I'd hoped that Francis would just abandon me as soon as I ran away, but he insisted on accompanying me to a chair against the far wall. He told me to sit down and relax while he got me something to drink. Eagerly awaited a tall scotch, neat. Disappointed to receive plain tap water, squalid.

He handed it to me and threw himself on a ratty futon covered with old newspapers, saying, "I've never seen you wear pants before."

"Not 'pants.' Trousers. Pleats and cuffs."

A maddening black eyebrow shot upward. "Am I wearing pants?"

How to explain the nuances of modern menswear to a slacker? He can't appreciate anything but pumpkin-farmer jeans. Looked around at other offending garments. Bev, over by the hot dog rotisserie, wore polyester slacks in a janitorial hue. Her floral smock, three sizes too small, displayed a white roll of flesh spilling over an exhausted elastic waistband. Most of the techies draped themselves in ill-fitting denim, faded and stretched hipwise from sedentary years in the Hole. Other Jeff was the exception; he wore true pants, mercerized cotton with a sickly sheen that cruelly showed us the way God made him.

"Thought you were thirsty," said Francis.

I pretended to take a sip of the murky water and banged my bucks on the rim. I will never be able to afford quality braces. The NAL dental plan calls orthodontia "cosmetic dentistry" and won't cover it. As if! I'm only looking out for my health, trying to avoid jabbing shards of filthy glass into my gums and bleeding to death. Everyone knows I haven't a vain bone in my body.

Francis leaned back on his elbow, stretching his legs out. His eyes were upon my trousers. He was probably sick with envy over the Little Frenchman's excellent wool-blend tailoring.

"You should wear your glasses more often," he said. "They make you look smart."

I adjusted the wretched spectacles on my nose. I am into those huge, round Jackie O frames, but the NAL doesn't offer an optical plan. I have been wearing these *My Three Sons* glasses for ten years.

"In fact," he went on, "with your bangs matted down like that you look like Aus—"

I interrupted this painful simile, as I have endured it from Val for three years and cannot take any more. Matted! Anyone with sense knows my bangs are *slicked* down in elfin points à la Mia Farrow circa 1968.

"I think I might need something a bit stronger," I said, returning the water to him, "like a double scotch. Or just bring the bottle. Please." He muttered something about rudeness, grabbed the glass out of my hand with force, and stalked off. Rude? Not me; I said please. He must have been apologizing for his rudeness in comparing me to Austin Powers. It was time to give Fat Bald Jeff his birthday present. He was taking a break from the Foghat to load up on beer.

"Don't you want to open your present?" I asked, waving the package in front of his nose.

"Love to," he said. He swilled the rest of his brew. It was disgusting, watching the beer slosh over the rim and down his chin, yet I found it an impressive display of alcohol capacity.

He ripped off the company-letterhead wrapping paper, then stroked his moist chin thoughtfully. He seemed pleased and said it would come in handy when drafting poison-pen letters.

We sat down on two milk crates near the front of the loft. I had never sat on a milk crate before. I asked him about the excruciating dog in the front yard. He said, "It's a long story."

Fat Bald Jeff had moved into the shanty five years ago. His landlady, a Miss Havisham-like lunatic who floats about the stairwells in her nightgown carrying candles, offered him the room for two hundred dollars a month. Her son, the occupant of the first floor and mongrel owner, used to utilize the attic for parties and certain business transactions. Jeff didn't say what kind of transactions, but one can only draw the conclusion of the drug trade! Wicked, yet very thrilling. The son resents the intrusion on his lifestyle and encourages the mongrel to lunge at Jeff whenever he comes in or out.

"Has it ever bitten you?" I asked.

"Once," he said. "But I was heavier then and stuck out more into the yard when I came down the walk. As long as I can keep my weight down to two-fifty, it can't reach me."

This was *loads* more exciting than old Paco smoking butts on our front stoop in his velour jogging suit.

I looked around the loft. Poster of Shatner (pregirdle), dorm fridge, old futon dressed in stiff brownish sheets, gold-tone picture frame with photo of his mother (not too fat, but a little bald), collection of samurai swords on the wall, extensive computer setup, milk crates full of identical black clothes. Despite having no electrical outlets and hunching around under the eaves of an attic and the general state of squalor, Jeff seemed content. A resilient thing, the human being. Why, I myself had to abide the uncomfortable Edith Bunker chair, not to mention the vegetable crisper in the fridge, which slides shakily on a warped runner! I suppose I will become hardened by these trials, but when Martin and I move up the privileged ranks, I will remember retrieving rotten lime rinds from behind the garbage can and buying rail drinks at the bar, and I will be a little wiser, a little more compassionate toward the beggars hounding the fence at our gated community.

Suddenly Francis materialized at my left. Out of breath and perspiring, he plunked down a bottle of J&B on the floor.

"Where'd you get that?" asked Jeff.

"You didn't have any scotch, so I ran to the liquor store two blocks away and bought some."

"Ugh," replied Jeff. "*That* place. The clerk always harasses me. Did he give you a hard time?"

"Yes. In fact, he shortchanged me and we got in a big argument. Then a cop showed up and told me to get lost, and I never got the right change back." He looked at me expectantly. "Well, have at it, Addie."

I glanced at the bottle sorrowfully. "No Chivas?"

Francis stormed off into the dancing crowd while Fat Bald Jeff collapsed in gales of laughter. I don't see what's so funny about preferring decent liquor. I choked down a third of the bottle over half an hour or so, then finally slammed it down in disgust. J&B is quite undrinkable.

Went off in search of the bathroom. Could it be that Jeff didn't even have plumbing? After a circuit around the perimeter of the loft, I finally asked someone for directions. He pointed me to the center of the room. In a sort of magnetic horror, I was pulled toward a dilapidated structure surrounded by a translucent shower curtain. In the middle stood a toilet and creepy metal bathtub. A person moved about inside, almost completely visible to those outside! Why not rig up a spotlight over it? Transfixed, I gawked openly.

"It's rude to stare," barked Bev as she emerged from behind the curtain.

The room began to spin as I recoiled in terror. Shall I ever banish from my memory the vision of Bev performing her natural functions? I turned around and stumbled into a group of computer nerds. As I passed out of consciousness, I was tossed back and forth, as though none of them wanted to touch me!

I remember rasping, "Get . . . help . . ." at the reluctant technicians. Oh, and I also remember eventually being lowered onto the futon by greasy hands as I writhed helplessly and mumbled, "Dry-clean blouse . . . no touch." To no avail!

Sometime later, I awoke. It was quiet and dark. I drifted along in a pleasant semiconscious state until a whiff of soiled linens assaulted my nostrils. Jeff's futon! I tried to sit up, but hands gently pushed me back down, urging me to rest. Dizziness returned.

Monstrous, nightmarish images passed before me. The grizzled mongrel snapping its jaws. A nine-hundred-pound bicycle strapped to my back. Dancing technicians. Bottles of half-empty J&B, surrounding me like a crop circle. Massive underpants and iron-gray bangs. Dirty fingerprints on a cream silk blouse.

"My God!" I sobbed, sitting bolt upright. "It's a *Christian Lacroix*!"

"Who?" someone whispered.

"I don't know," came an answer. "Is she delirious?"

Bloblike forms emerged. Dark hair, impish eyebrows, blue eyes, pumpkin-farmer jeans. A fat, bald head. Pounding commenced at my temples and reality flooded in. Jeff and Francis hovered over me anxiously as I struggled to rally. They said I was dehydrated, had had too much to drink and fainted. As if mere *alcohol* induced my nausea! I know the truth: agony this miserable could only be caused by the sight of Bev issuing forth from an open-air commode.

"Why does it have to be in the middle of the room?" I pleaded with Jeff. "Why do the curtains have to be clear? A prison toilet has more dignity."

They ignored my ramblings as they helped me down the fire escape. Francis insisted on driving me home. Put on my plastic rain bonnet and driving goggles, slumped in the passenger seat, and dozed off. Next thing I knew, he was groping me at the front door.

"Unhand me," I cried weakly.

He threw me a disgusted look. "I'm trying to find your keys."

The goggles had begun to steam up, and the rain bonnet slid forward over them. Trapped by my own accoutrements and unable to find my keys, I pressed our buzzer until Val Wayne came down the stairs.

Francis gave him the rundown on my condition, and they had a bloody good laugh as they dragged me up the stairs. I prayed that 2F would not hear all the ruckus. But, as usual, God mocked my request. Stefan and Chung opened the door and watched in stunned silence as the boys shoved me up the last flight. The rain bonnet slipped further, covering my mouth, and I began to hyperventilate. Through the fogged lenses I saw 2F exchange pitying glances. They will never accept me now.

"I need a nightcap," I moaned through the bonnet.

Val and Francis roughly pushed me in the apartment. Francis must have left about then, but I don't remember. Val helped me out of my clothes. With fading strength I feebly grabbed Val's shirt and whispered, "Hang up blouse." He recklessly threw it over an old wire hanger.

"*Padded satin* hanger . . ." I croaked, but he told me to shut up and go to sleep. Teared up at his carelessness. He knows I am fanatical about wrinkled garments. I drowsily muttered, "Christian Lacroix" as sleep stole over me.

"Austin Powers," he responded.

Moaned a bit at that, but Val merely turned off the light and shut the door behind him.

Chapter 6

Stayed home from work and watched religious television. I will never be swayed by those evangelists. They're always wearing white trousers. Grandmother says white trousers are vulgar, unless one is playing croquet.

Val made me a soft-boiled egg before he went to work. I had dry toast with it and black coffee. I had asked for breakfast in bed, but he said he was my roommate, not my mother. That's ridiculous. Everyone knows my mother can't boil an egg properly.

Felt sorry for Val as he groomed himself before work. His mustache was a disgrace. It detracted from his otherwise neat appearance.

"What's a paralegal do, anyway?" I asked.

He said he spent a lot of time in the company coat closet with one of the lawyers. I recalled my secret meeting with Fat Bald Jeff in *our* company coat closet, which can barely admit a raincoat, let alone two impassioned zombies. That's what you get working for a nonprofit.

"I have an idea," I said, and led Val into the bathroom. I offered him three shades of eyebrow pencil—black, brown-black, and sable.

"What's this for?" he asked. I looked sadly at his half 'stache.

"Oh," he said. He chose the sable.

Afterward, he surveyed his results in the medicine-cabinet mirror. Not a bad job, but I had to restrain him from filling in whiskers below the corners of his mouth.

"It's very nice," I said. "You look like Prince." Val frowned for a second, as he considers Prince a nancy boy, then admitted that he was an excellent guitarist. Perhaps, but he is still no Lionel Richie.

Called early and left a message on Coddles's voice mail, telling him I was ill. If we speak to him live when calling in sick, he tries to convince us to come in to work. Planned on staying in pajamas all day. Strolled about the empty apartment feeling leisurely. Watched the video of Yanni's Acropolis concert and realized that Yanni's mother (seated next to Linda Evans) was also crying! This observation made me cry a little, too. Yanni is one good-looking Greek pianist, and it's a shame he's throwing it all away on the washed-up star of *Dynasty*.

At ten-thirty Francis phoned to ask how I was feeling. It was hard to be offhanded about the previous night's activities. I've never really fainted before, except for one time when the Lemming took me to see the Lyric Opera's production of *Tristan and Isolde*. It was very moving. Anyway, I told Francis I would need plenty of rest if I was to recover my former vigor. I could not stand another round of heckling; so I fell down in Jeff's hovel and hyperventilated through my rain bonnet, so what? Dean Martin fell off the stage at the Sands countless times, and everyone said he was absolutely charming.

The Lemming called in the midst of a Saltines and ginger-ale binge.

"What are you doing home in the middle of the day?" he accused.

"Why are you calling here in the middle of the day?" I shot back, choking on the crackers. The Lemming and I parry barbs like an old married couple. Can't he see we belong together, bound by law and expensive gold rings?

"What's wrong with your voice? You sound like you're retching," he said.

"I'm convalescing," I said. Why elaborate on the cause? Even though the Lemming appreciates good liquor, he might be loath to take on a fiancée who falls down drunk at parties.

He said, "Well, I just wanted to leave a message to ask if you were available tonight, but I guess not." I *would* be available to accept four carats, but not available to help him do his laundry, which is what he had planned for us this evening. Nerve!

By lunchtime I had started to feel like my old self again. So much better, in fact, that I began to feel like I was playing hooky from the Place—which is scads more enjoyable than merely missing work due to illness. This elevated my mood considerably, so I switched off religious television and got dressed. Since no one was about, I put on a pair of pumpkin-farmer pants and a green cotton sweater. Caught a glimpse of myself in the mirror. Looked gaseous, but nothing like Austin Powers.

Went out in the yard. The boys had dug a large bed in the back, with curved edges that ran down along one side of our fence. Massive bags of peat moss, cow manure, and humus sat by the garage in readiness. The peat moss disbursed a ripe, earthy pungency that smelled wonderful outside. It also emitted a reeking fetor when thoroughly embedded in pristine wheat overalls. Felt a mean sort of satisfaction the other night at the sight of 2F's gardening clothes hanging up in the laundry room, filthy and stinky even after several washings.

A separate square bed had been dug in the corner, probably for vegetables. Val said he wanted to plant an olive tree for our martinis, but I said our climate was all wrong. I had then waited for him to ask what *I* would like to plant, but he just said he'd consider planting cocktail onions instead. Grandmother would be very impressed with the boys' effort. As for myself, I was simply a cynical observer. Until they invited me to participate, I could only look on with amused detachment.

Teared up a bit when I thought of Gran's lovely cottage garden. She *cannot* be as infirm as she says! She still wears spectator pumps to church. We still do the Sunday crossword puzzle together over the phone each week. She still arranges her hair into a neat chignon and puts full makeup on every day, even when she just sits around the house playing solitaire. Old people do none of these things. They stare at peeling walls and think their maids are stealing from them.

If Gran is indeed becoming frail and incontinent, then it is no one's fault but my parents'. Decades of witnessing their free-living experiments and hideola clothing have undoubtedly broken down Gran's resistance to disease. Her decline really started the day we left on our cross-country bus trip. Father drove the VW minibus over to my grandparents' house so we could say good-bye. Grandmother stood in the driveway, flapping a funeral fan and clutching at Grandfather. Father exited the bus, shirtless in front of his own mother! Admittedly, he did wear a giant brass KEEP ON TRUCKIN' belt buckle that covered half his stomach, so at least they were spared the vision of his crusty navel and gruesome "happy trail." Grandfather staggered backward a step or two as Mother jumped out of the bus to hug him good-bye. She wore a see-through macramé vest, blue Janis Joplin sunglasses, and low-rise, flared jeans that looked lousy on her childbearing hips. My parents had ordered me to stay in the bus, but I made my escape as they tried to wheedle gas money out of Grandfather. Ran to Grandmother and flung myself at her bosom. She stumbled a bit, but hung on.

"Oh, Gran!" I cried. "Don't let them take me!" She hugged me tight as Grandfather squeezed my shoulder and made soothing sounds. Gran launched an almighty pair of poison darts from her eyes at Mother.

"Should we leave Addie here?" Mother asked Father. She *would*! The wistfulness in her voice was impossible to ignore.

But Father pulled me away. I struggled out of his grasp and threw myself into the azaleas. Neighbors had come out to watch the show. I gave a decent hysterical performance, which ended in anticlimax as Father drawled, "Is that the best you can do?" Could have done better, I suppose, but didn't want to scuff my shiny Mary Janes.

Grandfather sighed and pulled out his wallet. He counted out some bills for Father as Grandmother gently rolled me out of the bush.

"Darling, it's a delicate variety," she said. I wept into the mulch.

The neighbors shook their heads and went back home. "It's the mother I feel sorry for," muttered one of them. Meaning Gran, obviously.

Exhausted and spent, I trudged into the bus like a prisoner to the gallows. Gran handed me a box of six dozen chocolate bourbon-ball cookies in front of Mother and said it was likely that these would be the last home-cooked things I would eat for some time. Then when I seated myself in the back, she slipped me a pocket-size white book through the bus window.

"It's the Good Book," she whispered. "Read it in secret and don't let the heathens take it from you." I thumbed through it. She had highlighted all the passages about wanton women and motherless children. Gran and I waved our twin hankies at each other as Father drove down the street. She looked like a little old person.

For days we drove. The parents sang boring labor anthems while I surreptitiously scanned biblical passages. They were looking for a certain commune where people grew their own food and shared all their belongings, but they weren't sure if it was in Iowa or Oregon.

"I'm not sharing my underpants," I told Mother.

"Nobody wants those convent bedsheets," she snapped.

I cried. Mother never understood my need for modest undergarments. But some primal mothering instinct deep within her must have been activated by the sound of my sobs. Against her will, she stiffly petted my head and asked Father sotto voce what those little squeegee things were.

"Tears, I think," he said.

She handed me a greasy rag from the bus floor and said, "Blow."

It was just pure luck that I haven't turned out maladjusted.

* * *

Staring at the square that would soon be home to vegetable rows gave me a queasy feeling. I've nothing against vegetables. If it weren't for them, my digestion would be as sluggish as the Chicago sewers. And I liked helping Grandmother pick out veggies for her garden. But the experience of growing them has been ruined for me by Mother's pioneer efforts in hydroponic bus gardening. I shared the backseat with trays of pale cabbages and carrots, which jealously sucked all the nutrients out of my air. Even though I now understand the symbiotic relationship we have with plants, I am convinced that those particular weeds robbed me of vital pubescent nourishment. Nevertheless, I resumed speaking to the parents several days into the journey, to ask if I could grow some flowers.

"We don't have room to grow anything that we don't eat," said Father. My eyes strayed to the cannabis plant on the wheel well.

"You can eat that," he said, eyes flashing in a dangerous challenge. "Go ahead. Eat some." Peer pressure from my own father! I shook my head and replied that *one* of us had better stay lucid as we wove in and out of the highway lanes past state troopers. He turned back to his driving but anxiously checked the rearview mirror three hundred times over the next hour.

We drove through most of Iowa, ostensibly looking for the commune. I think they just liked traveling around because, as Father said, "everywhere is beautiful, man." Everywhere, that is, but Evanston, Illinois. What was wrong with Evanston? We had a civilized block club and timely garbage men.

We had left on our trip at the end of August, and as the September days passed on, I asked my parents if we would be back in time for my first day of eighth grade at St. Cuthbert's.

"You're not going back to St. Cuthbert's," they said. "We're homeschooling you in the bus."

I fell upon my hard sleeping pallet and wailed. My whole world—gone! Gone was the prim, starched little uniform I so loved. Gone was the possibility that this year I would make a school friend. Gone were the lessons in Catholic Doctrine, English Composition, and U.S. History—to be replaced with Beginning Tai Chi, Communism as a Viable Alternative to the Pig System, Lying About 101, and—worst of all—Open-mike Poetry Readings.

I went on a hunger strike that was supplemented by private scarfing of Grandmother's bourbon balls, but nothing would make the parents turn back home. I woke up early one morning, three days into the strike, and found a blotchy red mess extending over my face, neck, and ears. I screamed as I glimpsed my reflection in the rearview mirror. Mother groggily sat up and rubbed her eyes.

"Look what you've done to me, Mother!" I shrieked. "Eczema. Psoriasis. Lupus. Major epidermal inflammation. All from living in this disgusting bus with no food and all these cabbages stealing my oxygen!"

She sighed and poked me in the face. "Zits."

I screamed again, for it was even worse than I had suspected.

Mother told me to be quiet, as Father was still asleep. Worn out, I expect, from long days of singing songs and not working. She began unearthing piles of garbage around the bus in search of Father's kit of homeopathic remedies.

I cried, "I don't want bovine udder salve or essence of bugloss smeared on my face. I want chemicals and I want them now." She ignored me and withdrew an empty cardboard box that was hidden under my straw pallet.

"You ate seventy-two cookies in three days? No wonder you look like you've had an acid bath."

I slumped down in the passenger seat and whimpered that I had been starving to death. She made disparaging remarks about the success of my hunger strike.

I stared at my gross countenance in the rearview mirror as she went back to her pallet. She'd given me a tub of creamy goat unguent to slather on my pustules. I openly refused this treatment, then glopped some on when she finally fell asleep again.

Bored and needing to go to the bathroom, I sneaked out of the bus. I thought we had passed by a public library recently but couldn't remember which way to go. I was always disoriented, since we had to move our bus every night. The Iowans complained about our eyesore of a vehicle parked on their quaint streets. Father didn't see anything wrong with parking the hunk of junk in front of people's houses, then napping on their lawns.

"It's everybody's planet," he objected.

After wandering around for an hour—where I could have been abducted by a depraved Iowan, no thanks to my parents—I found the library. Immediately reassured by the air-conditioning and asbestos tiles, I heaved a sigh of relief. *This* was more like it. I walked in the bathroom and was struck dumb by the horrible little girl staring at me from the full-length mirror. The oozing skin condition was vile enough. It was the rest that pushed me over the edge.

My hair hung in two lank plaits, dripping like the grease trap at a Chinese restaurant. Half-moons of dirt adorned each quick-bitten fingertip. A ring of filth encircled my neck like an Elizabethan collar. My T-shirt—once snowy white with darling cap sleeves—was now sullied with chocolate bourbon thumbprints, and the iron-on decal was coming loose from the fabric. My shorts exposed a shockingly defiled pair of knees. Black scabs on the shins, threadbare tennis shoes. And I stank. My God, how I still remember that smell: like a can of bacon drippings forgotten under the sink.

I, who had always prided myself on a conventional appearance, now looked for all the world like a common guttersnipe.

Twenty minutes later, as I scrubbed myself raw with a hard little nub of yellow soap and brown paper towels, I began to emerge from my stench. I had to leave on the goat ointment in order to clear up my skin, but the rest of me was in better shape. The shirt was still dirty, but as Mother had given up laundry as a tool of masculine oppression, I would have to live with it.

Exited the bathroom and headed toward the stacks. A good hour or so with kindred spirit Oliver Twist would restore me. How I longed for a nice tidy orphanage with good-tasting porridge! But I hardly had time to consider Fagan's unseemly attachment to cockney boys when a bony finger jabbed me in the shoulder.

It was the librarian, asking why I wasn't in school. Confused, I tried in vain to recall St. Cuthbert's start date, then remembered I wasn't going back there at all. I hurriedly explained that my parents were homeschooling me in a bus, but with a sweeping glance, she took in my scullery duds and DOWN WITH THE PIG SYSTEM decal and promptly called the truancy office. Curse Mother and her stinking forays into politics! The only time she had ever wielded an iron was to solder that horrid patch to my shirt.

The truant officer sequestered me in a small cataloging room in the back and barraged me with questions and insults, as though I had swiped a lipstick at Woolworth's. He wanted a phone number where he could reach my parents, but I explained that our bus had no phone line nor even electricity for household cleaning appliances. He demanded to be taken to the bus, but I couldn't remember where it was.

The truant officer and I drove around for two hours and finally found the bus on a quiet suburban street four blocks away. We pulled up in front of it and watched Mother and Father roll about on someone's lawn like two vulgar teenagers, apparently unconcerned with their missing child. The truant officer started barking things at my parents. My father jumped up and starting barking things back. He was wearing a paisley loincloth.

We all had to go down to the truancy office so my parents could explain their unorthodox schooling methods. More barking. Father called them "school pigs." Mother whispered that I smelled bad and told me to wipe off the goat salve.

It was dusk by the time we got back to the bus. Parents were screaming at each other and at me. We ate a silent meal of cold lentils in the bus. I cried into my bowl, then retreated to my bunk, where I commenced a fresh round of weeping into my indestructible hemp pillow. I could hear Mother and Father talking quietly outside the bus, and I wailed louder. Sometime later they came to me, grasped my hands, and looked meaningfully into my eyes. I perceived a turning point. Had they reclaimed their senses and decided to drive back home? There was still time to iron my kneesocks and rehem my uniform.

"Addie," began Mother in a solemn voice, "Dad and I have been talking. We appreciate what you've given up to travel the country with us, and we want to show you how grateful we are. It's a big deal to come of age on the road."

Uneasily, I sensed a group discussion of menstruation.

But Father said with the air of one passing down Hammurabi's Code of Indulgences, "Yes, hon. We want you to call us Harvey and Ruth."

Kicked and screamed until the morning light.

Fat Bald Jeff phoned later on. He was breathless and difficult to understand. He said he was calling from the Italian joint next door to the Place.

"Why didn't you call from the Hole?" I asked.

"I couldn't risk being overheard!"

Ha! Everyone knows the other techies could not bother rousing interest in anything besides motherboards, Hot Dog Day, and the annual party in the boiler room celebrating Leonard Nimoy's birthday. But Jeff assured me that he had ample reason for discretion.

"Well, out with it," I said, impatient for the news. I had an instant onion soup in the microwave.

"I can't say," he replied. "It's a matter of security. But can I stop by after work to talk to you?"

There's nothing like fat, bald melodrama. But I looked forward to Val's meeting Jeff. He knew all about Jeff's hovel and degradation from my description over soft-boiled eggs this morning.

About five o'clock I heard the pitiful cries of the puppy on the fire escape across the gangway. I peeked out Val's bedroom window. It was sitting in its cage and shivering. A soft rain had started, adding to the pathetic tableau. Sat down on Val's bed and thought. Decided I could either call some animal organization, send a strongly worded note to the owners, or ask Val to intimidate the owners with menacing threats. Letters of complaint are my forte, but I didn't think they would have much effect in this situation. It's not like the dog owners are the CTA, in danger of losing my business forever. And Val, frankly, is not very menacing-looking, with his burnout glasses and Beatle boots and particolored sportswear. He also has a velvet frock coat that he struts about in every autumn, much to the delight of the neighborhood. No, I would have to phone the officials.

The officials, however, were less than forthcoming. They said they needed substantial evidence to investigate. I pointed out that the puppy cried all the time—one doesn't cry all the time unless one is mistreated. I should know! I spent two and a half years crying inconsolably on the minibus. But the animal official merely said she would process my complaint and that I should call back in a week's time.

"In a week's time, it may be too late," I warned.

"Ten days, then," she said and hung up. Curse our dispassionate system!

The buzzer sounded. Ah, Jeff. He would know what to do about the puppy. He had a lot of experience with both neglected mongrels and indifferent bureaucrats.

But after I hit the buzzer and opened my door, I found Francis standing there, holding a bunch of drippy red carnations.

"Don't you ask who's there when people ring your buzzer?" he asked. I said I was expecting someone else.

"Oh, well, I won't stay long," he said, pushing his way in and sitting down in the Edith Bunker chair. I stared in dismay at the wet footprints that followed him. He caught my gaze and hurriedly dropped to his knees to sop up the puddles with his sleeve. I took the flowers from him so he could utilize the full advantage of both sleeves.

"Carnations," I said, beaming appreciatively. "A most economical choice."

He looked up. "The florist said all flowers have meanings, and she suggested these when I described you to her."

I went to the kitchen to put them in water and stole a quick glance at an old book of mine on the Victorian meanings of flowers: *Red carnation—Alas! my poor heart.* The florist must have a different translation.

We chatted for a while. Never had a conversation before whilst wearing pumpkin-farmer pants—I suppose I can be as shocking and audacious as the next girl! Felt like a devil-may-care beat poet. The doorbell sounded again, and

I jumped up to buzz Jeff in. Unfortunately, opening the door revealed a damp and peevish Lemming. He, too, held a small bouquet of flowers—anemones and filler sprigs of barberry.

"Raining," he grouched. He stepped in, glanced at Francis sitting placidly in the corner, and turned to me with a look as black as thunder.

"Sick, are you?"

"Convalescing," I said.

Francis stood up and introduced himself while I ran to look for another vase. I'd already used the good one for the red carnations, so I had to use the hideous clay one fashioned by my father. Roaches and fingernail clippings were sealed in the glaze. I skimmed *The Language of Flowers* for the meaning of the Lemming's nosegay. It said sickness and sourness of temper. Grabbed a roll of paper towels and ran back to the living room, where I thrust the vase at Martin and moodily wiped up the wet trail that led from door to disco couch.

"Oh, shall I help?" Martin offered weakly, rising a half inch from the couch.

"No, no. It's nothing. Just talk amongst yourselves while I mop this up and wax the floor."

I was crouched on all fours, scrubbing, when the door suddenly swung open and bonked me on the head.

"Oops!" said Val Wayne. I sat rubbing my head while Val hung up his coat and quietly studied the scene around him: I, attired in perverse pumpkin pants, slavishly mopping the floor with inferior towelettes; the Lemming, moistly glowering on the disco couch; Francis, nervously pulling at his rampant brows; and two vases of calumny sitting on the coffee table.

A smile slowly eased itself under his penciled 'stache, which was smeared somewhat from the rain. "I was going to meet a friend for coffee, but I think I'll stay home after all."

He whistled as he went in the kitchen to mix us all some drinks.

By the time the buzzer sounded again, I had finished the second coat of wax and crawled feebly to the intercom.

"Who is it?" I asked warily.

"It's Fat Bald Jeff."

Never thought I'd thank God for the arrival of Fat Bald Jeff.

He carried my bicycle up to the third floor and seemed put out when I told him it belonged in the basement. He needs the exercise, and anyway, my health is far too delicate at present to be carting bicycles up and down stairs like a common laborer. Well, we were all quite chummy, the five of us, after a round of drinks in the living room. Francis sat stiffly in the Edith Bunker chair, taking minuscule sips of Ouzo out of a hollowed-out coconut. The Lemming sat like a fop, feet tucked underneath him on the disco couch, and drank vodka with pink lemonade from the chipped-rim Miami Dolphins tumbler. Val and I sat on the couch too, with G&Ts in sordid ceramic vessels (fired by Father) in the shape of obscene orchids. Fat Bald Jeff sat on the floor and drank beer out of an I ♥ GRANDPA mug. Val offered to pull a folding chair out of our storage closet for Jeff, but the stout man said not to bother. I imagine he's used to sitting on floors.

Went in the kitchen to top off my drink. Val followed.

"I, for one, am interested in seeing what comes of this freakish gathering," he said.

I peeked down the hall into the living room. "No one dares move," I whispered.

"Why is the fat, bald one here?"

"He's bringing me something from work. Didn't you see the manila envelope he's clutching in his lap?"

"Oh, yeah," said Val, "he growled at me when I reached down to refill his mug."

We walked back in with our drinks, and then Val Wayne Newton made an utterly wicked suggestion.

"Say, let's get out of here. We can all go in my car." I looked apprehensively from one face to another. Francis's features tightened and his Adam's apple convulsed frighteningly; the Lemming squared his weak jaw and a white dent appeared on either side of his nose; Fat Bald Jeff made spasmodic movements with his eyebrows and darted his eyes repeatedly from me to the manila envelope. A grin as wide as Jeff's midriff stretched across Val's smug face. I gulped the contents of my orchid.

We trudged after Val, single file, to the garage. He opened his London Fog umbrella, as he needed to protect his mustache from further running. He barely made room for me under it, but I forced my way in. The Lemming squealed and complained about the weather, but the other two silently tramped in the rain. I expect they're accustomed to inconvenience and discomfort. Val and Jeff sat in the front seat, while I sat between Francis and Martin in the back. Thankfully, there was no need for conversation, as Val had Metallica playing full volume in the CD player. Francis began to bobble his head wildly to the music, while the Lemming flinched with each boom of the kick drum. Jeff seemed unaware that there was even any music on. No one asked where we were going.

We pulled up outside Myopic Books, a used bookstore and café. Val got a cup of coffee and immediately disappeared to a table in the back, where one of his tarts sat brooding, with crossed arms and pouting lips. So he kept his coffee date after all and merely brought the men along to torment me!

As the Lemming ordered himself an espresso, Francis took advantage and pulled me over to the activists' bulletin board. He pointed to a flyer with a picture and a caption that read FREE MUMIA ABU-JAMAL, and recited the facts of an exciting conspiracy to me. I remarked that in the seventies my mother's hair looked just like Mumia's.

Fat Bald Jeff tugged at my sleeve, shook the manila envelope violently, and whispered, "We have our *own* conspiracy here, if you don't mind."

The Lemming suddenly appeared at our side, sipping his espresso waspishly.

"Guilty," said the Lemming.

Francis whirled about. "How can you say that? He was framed!"

"Isn't it suspicious that he was driving his cab by the exact location, at the exact time, where a cop was beating up his brother?"

"The cop's brother?" I asked.

"*Mumia's* brother," the Lemming answered.

"And someone shot him," continued Francis.

"Mumia?" I asked.

"The cop's brother?" questioned Jeff, now getting in on the act.

"There is no cop's brother!"

"So someone shot him—" repeated Francis.

"Mumia," I explained to Jeff.

"No one shot Mumia. Mumia killed the cop," said the Lemming.

"Mumia *did* get shot, but Mumia did *not* kill the cop," retorted Francis.

"Is Mumia okay?" asked Jeff.

Francis scoffed, "If you call a death sentence okay!"

"Well, the cop's *dead*," said the Lemming.

"Who shot the cop?" I asked.

"Exactly!" they both shouted, glaring at each other.

I screamed out, "Third base!" No one laughed.

I disappeared into the mystery section to escape further rancor. I picked up a paperback of *Ten Little Indians.* It's one of Gran's favorite books, but I've never read it. It always seemed common, having been made into a movie with Fabian and so on. I handed over the money and asked for a glass of cold water.

The clerk tried to charge me a quarter, but I refused to pay. Comments were made. What kind of nut pays for water? Walking away from the counter, I thumbed through the book and realized whole pages were torn out from the end of the book.

"Hey, look at this! The last chapter's missing! What kind of bookstore is this?" I said loudly. People turned to look while the clerk turned red.

I demanded a different copy. The clerk rummaged around in the stacks for a while, muttering obscenities, no doubt, then came back and shoved another paperback at me.

"Are you sure this is a different copy?" I asked doubt-fully. "Because I can't stand—"

The floor began to quake as Jeff came stomping up be-hind me, sneaky as a Pamplona bull, and tapped me on the shoulder. "Addie, you've got to see what I have here. National Association of Libraries scandal and smut."

"I'm in the middle of—did you say 'smut'?"

But just then Francis came up and ordered a coffee, so Jeff grimaced and walked away.

Francis stirred sugar into his mug and cast an unfriendly glance in the Lemming's direction. "Phew! Who *is* that guy?"

It isn't easy explaining my relationship with Martin, as I am not sure of it myself.

Francis listened and looked both shocked and amused. "That despot is your boyfriend?"

"Well, one man's despot is another man's boyfriend," I said limply, but it didn't convey quite the right meaning. We went over to Val and his vixen's table. She was sitting on his lap, so I took her chair. Francis, encouraged by our discussion on Mumia, gave tongue to his favorite issues: political pris-oners and the death penalty.

"You see," he began, "Mumia symbolizes our society's mass criminalization of black males and the bipartisan pro-gram for quicker executions with fewer appeals. He's on death row and we're fighting for his appeal, not only for his own sake but for the sake of human rights."

I said, "But if he's on death row, isn't he guilty?"

Francis just looked at me sadly. He explained our rot-ten criminal justice system and how often the innocent lan-guish in jail cells. He said, "Consider Leonard Peltier. Fred

Hampton, Junior. Rolando Cruz. Victims of a corrupt police state."

After reflecting on my impasse with the animal official, I felt I understood how an innocent creature could slip though the cracks. Vowed to become more revolutionary. Francis went on about his other political concerns: hemp, PVC, Dow Chemical, the drug war, dry cleaning.

"I like animals. I am into animal rights," I said.

Like a butler wearing wrestling shoes, the Lemming materialized out of nowhere. "Oh, you like animals, do you, Addie? What kind? Or should I say, how do you like them prepared?"

Visions of sole Véronique and beef tenderloin danced before me. My mouth watered guiltily. "Martin, I adore animals! Dogs and cats are especially, er . . . nice and good."

Francis confided that he ate meat too. Val and the trollop disappeared under the table and Martin took their chair.

"So, Francis, tell me," he said with a crabbed little smile, "what do you do?"

Francis looked uncomfortable and began to pull at his eyebrows. "I'm a graphic designer."

I'd never noticed before how tight the Lemming's collars were, or how his face flushed a disgusting shade whenever he approached some pet subject with dreary passion.

"A graphic delinquent! How nice." The men sized up each other like economists at a collegiate debate. I chewed my nails down to bleeding stubs. Francis coughed dryly and corrected him.

"Oh, that's right," replied the Lemming. "You're an *artist*." He invested the word with its full quota of sinister significance.

I escaped to the front of the store, where I found Fat Bald Jeff perusing the *Star Trek* section. I sat on the stepladder in the aisle, trembling.

"I think I'm having a digestive disturbance," I said. "My prescribed dinner hour was thirty minutes ago."

"Speaking of disturbances," said Jeff, "take a look here." He removed a photograph from his precious envelope and showed it to me.

I frowned at the picture. "All I can see are two Santa hats."

"So the picture's a little dark. I can fix that. The Santa hats are attached to Gladys, the marketing VP, and Carlson in accounting."

Oh. *Oh!* Zombies in flagrante delicto!

I groaned. "Jeff, I don't feel so good."

"I know," he sympathized. "It made me sick too." I put my head between my knees as he whispered his plans for the picture. Could hardly process his words as my stomach lurched and tiny *Enterprise*s flew round my head. I heard Francis and Martin approaching and groaned again.

"Too much gin," I croaked. "Need . . . fiber . . ." Someone ran to the counter, and the next thing I knew, a bran muffin was stuffed in my mouth.

"Maybe she's hypoglycemic," I heard Francis say.

Val appeared in the haze, snorting. "Maybe she's a hypochondriac."

Val torments me even as I hover between life and death.

Rode home in the Buick Electra, stretched out in the backseat. I wanted to stay at the bookstore, but my agony annoyed the other customers. In the car I tried to be brave, but groaning was so much easier. I peeked at the back of *Ten Little Indians.* Again, pages were missing! It was the exact same book! But this time the clerk had written on the inside back cover: *It was the judge. The end.*

Groaned more. I rested my feet on Francis and my head in Martin's lap. Reminded me of something awful involving Andrew Lloyd Webber and lobster thermidor at the Pump Room, but luckily passed out before remembering what. Vaguely recalled the boys lifting me up the three flights of our apartment building. Vaguely recalled a lot of grumbling and complaining. I weigh only 107 pounds, so it can't be that.

Passed 2F, who opened their door to watch the parade. I smiled bravely at them, but they shut the door in the midst of my suffering.

"Just put her anywhere," said Val as we entered our home. They dumped me on the disco couch. Fat Bald Jeff pressed the stinking manila envelope to my chest.

"We start tomorrow," he whispered and waddled out the door with the others.

Finally looked through the contents of the envelope. All I can say is, *Oh mama!*

Chapter 7

Coddles caught me playing solitaire this morning. He was tipped off by the gray behemoth in the cubicle next door. As he scolded me, I saw steel-wool bangs gopher over the top of the partition and heard a crude, screeching laugh, much like a wolverine devouring a litter of baby mice. Coddles should be glad I even showed up today. My digestion is completely off and my morale is at an all-time low after being carried up the stairs to my apartment twice in two nights.

"Your work level has been slow and unsatisfactory lately, Miss Prewitt," Coddles said, eyeing my bosom. "The Web project is moving along nicely, but that doesn't give you the right to shirk off your other duties."

He tramped out, and I turned to a dull manuscript on the productivity of teamwork in library management. A sentence in one of the articles read, "The highest level of success is achieved by workers who don't insist on being individuals, but rather teammates." I changed "teammates" to "zombies," printed out the final copy, and sent it off to the printer. What have I done? I suppose my unthinking obeisance has reached the breaking point. Perhaps Fat Bald Jeff's manila envelope of filth has destroyed what willingness I had to belong to the Place and complete my meaningless tasks on time. Perhaps work-centered society is to blame for not appreciating us peons. Perhaps my parents have ruined me for plebeian life with their flouting of convention. At any rate, I am now a useless member of the work force.

At 12:04, Fat Bald Jeff appeared at my cubicle opening and said, "Let's eat lunch outside. It's sunny." True, it was one of those glorious April days that usually sent me running for my trowel and blue gingham gauchos, but I'd lost my enthusiasm for the earth as well as for spring fashions. Why *not* trudge about in sackcloth and ashes like the parents wanted? I suppose the yucko pumpkin pants will be my uniform from now on.

He dragged me out to the industrial park across the street. Big squares of cement were lined up formally around a dead fountain, representing trees and other foreign objects. I sighed and opened up my bag. My lunch was completely beige: wheat bread with sliced tofurkey and mayo, butter beans, two stale sandwich cookies. Jeff's lunch, on the other hand, looked like the turnout from a successful food drive: pizza, steak and cheese sandwich, Mello Yello, bananas, Bun and Zero, fudge-covered granola bars, grapes, and a hot dog in a thermos. I tried to initiate a conversation, but he silenced me by holding up one fat finger, indicating digestion before discussion. I indicated by example that one should chew each mouthful thirty-two times, not twice. He disregarded my advice.

Finally, he brought out a copy of the disgusting material he had given me yesterday.

"What should we do with it?" I asked. "Notify the authorities?"

"The authorities?" he scoffed. "*We* are the authorities. We have the evidence, after all. That puts us in a position of authority, or power, anyway. What do you say to a secret, untraceable website detailing their activities?"

Suddenly, the sun broke through my miserable haze. Birds chirped on the cement blocks. The homeless men snoozing in the dead fountain became nomadic warriors. Dandelions pushing up through the cracks in the sidewalk appeared as prize-winning dahlias, searching for light. This plan of Jeff's could start me on my way to becoming revolutionary. My place at the Place all at once had some meaning.

"Like a scandal sheet? A gossip column? Grist for the rumor mill?" I asked.

"Yes"—he smiled happily—"except it's all true."

I looked again at the material: high-ranking zombies in various states of compromise. It seemed like everyone at last year's Christmas party had, at some point, stolen down to the dungeon and violated themselves on the floor. Grainy photos proved it. There were computer printouts of questionable charges on the corporate credit card, and heading the list was dear old Coddles.

"What's a Shirley Poppy, model four-five-nine?" I asked, looking at the first item.

Jeff replied, "A blowup doll," then went into sordid detail.

Ha! Who's shirking off *now*, Coddles?

"And don't overlook the items he purchased off the Internet from the Adult Happy-Nappy Corporation. They deal in intimate products for the contemporary infantilist."

I stared. "You mean . . . ?"

He nodded. "Gets off on wearing diapers and sucking on a pacifier while his secretary changes him." Hence the closed-door lunch meetings with Miss Fernquist each week!

"And he's not the only one," he said. He went on to show me the itemized corporate credit card report that listed the executives' annual purchases: airline trips, clothing from Neiman Marcus, and bills of sale from various salons and spas, among other things not usually paid for by one's employer. The bigwigs at the National Association of Libraries were as corrupt as television evangelists.

The day sped by. Received a phone call from Mother, anguishing over the lumbering Swede.

"Mother," I interrupted, "can't we talk later? I'm very busy at work. Don't you think I do anything here?"

She said dryly, "I know what you do there," and hung up. I switched off solitaire.

Fat Bald Jeff came to collect me at five o'clock. We were going to his hovel to plan the website. He said he had kept a secret network connection to the Place from his home computer for two years and could access all the information off the private financial reports and confidential personnel files.

"Not so private and confidential, eh?" he said with a wink. I am relieved that Jeff's on my side.

We exited the building, and I'm sure we made a merry sight climbing aboard the stinking Chicago Avenue bus. I had on a dowdy A-line rayon dress in prisoner-calming blue, matching gloves, and Cuban heels. It seemed the appropriate choice this morning as I agonized over my hangover. Jeff wore his usual T-shirt and denim mainsail jeans in slimming black. His motorcycle boots were scruffy and black. To accommodate his girth, he had added extra holes to his belt, possibly with his teeth. Also black. (Belt, not teeth. Teeth are yellow.) We sat in the front seat together, or rather he sat in the front seat and I folded myself into a greeting card next to the window.

I asked politely for an inch of room. He sighed irritably and shoved over.

"It's very bad for my coccyx to hang over the edge of the seat," he complained.

"Well, I certainly can't sit this way for more than a minute. My spine is not made of foam rubber."

Ended up sitting in his lap, which seemed the only reasonable thing to do. The other passengers snickered, but I think we held up our end of it with dignity.

"Let's get off here," he said. "We can pick up dinner on our way to my house."

I looked around for the café or urban market. But he led me to a disreputable-looking corner shanty. A baleful youth stood outside, looking us over. I clutched Jeff's pork-roast arm for reassurance, but he squirmed out of my grasp.

It was nothing more than a liquor store, and a shabby one at that!

"There's nothing to eat here," I whispered.

"Why are you whispering? Anyway, there's plenty to eat. Canned stuff down that aisle. Chips over here."

I sniffed distastefully. "It smells like rotting meat."

"See? I told you there was food."

I wandered around uncertainly. I found a bottle of Malibu Rum in the aisle marked BEAUTY AND HEALTH, but there was absolutely nothing edible for a person battling irritable bowel syndrome. I complained to Jeff, who said the only other place nearby for food was Chicken George, two doors down from the hovel. Chicken George had recently been under investigation for luring neighborhood cats into its back door, whence they were never seen again. I am a great lover of animals and could not possibly patronize such a place.

We approached the cashier, a sallow and crabby-looking Middle Eastern fellow, with our goods: rum and canned corn for me; Fanta grape soda, potato chips, baked beans, and Zingers for Jeff. When we got outside, Jeff grumbled that he had been shortchanged a dollar. I pointed out a police car parked right in front of the store, but he just told me to can it and pushed me along.

"In a neighborhood like this, poor, fat, bald guys have no friends," he muttered.

I said, "In what kind of neighborhood *do* they have friends?"

Struck by the sad eloquence of my words, we walked along in silence.

I tried to hold his hand, but he jerked it away. "I've got carpal tunnel syndrome," he said. "Do you mind?"

The hovel loomed before us like the Shanty of Usher. The grotesque mongrel strained at the end of its chain as Jeff stumped into its sight. On the front step sat a skinny man with long, tangled red hair, big gym sneakers with no shoelaces, snug white jeans, and a sleeveless shirt bearing the Rebel flag. I shook my head in disgust. Everyone knows it's too early in the season to wear white.

"Hey, fat boy," called the man. "I'm missing a bag of weed. You steal my weed, fatso?"

"I didn't steal your weed," replied Jeff in a tight voice as he scrunched by the growling dog. I clung to Jeff's shirt all the way down the sidewalk.

"Well, it's gone, right outta the garage. I saw you messin' around back there with some woman." He leered at me.

I cleared my throat. "Excuse me, I'm not his woman."

"Just shut up," hissed Jeff.

"Maybe I'll let Kong here search you for it." The animal yelped and twisted around at the sound of its name. Jeff and I had reached the building and continued down the walk toward the rear fire escape.

"Anyway, fat boy, my mama been lookin' for you," the man shouted after us. "You better pay your rent, fat boy, or Kong's gonna get real ugly." That's ridiculous. Dogs have no conception of real estate.

"Why me?" huffed Jeff.

We reached the top landing of the fire escape and he opened his door—whereupon an emaciated hag flew out of the loft and flung her broken twig arms around Fat Bald Jeff!

"Mrs. Nibbett!" he cried, disentangling himself from the hag.

She opened her mouth in a wide, frightening gap-toothed grin. "Oh Jeffy, I'm so glad you're safe! I was sick with worry, I tell you. Sick!"

"I'm all right," he said gruffly, "but you really shouldn't go in my apartment without my being there—"

"Oh Jeffy, what secrets are there between lovers?"

I would have staggered backward in amazement at this vaudevillian farce had we not been two and a half stories above their rotten yard.

"Mrs. Nibbett, I have to go inside now, okay?" said Jeff, inching by the harpy. He pulled me inside by the wrist, but before he could shut the door, she stuck her withered claw-foot in and jammed it open. She had a lot of strength for an animated corpse.

She breathed heavily, and up close I could see the layers of pancake makeup on her dry-onion skin. Where her lips must have once been were now just smears of frosty red, and silvery-blue eye shadow filled the sockets of her skull. Cotton-ball hair stood out in tufts from her scalp, and she wore a moth-eaten white nightgown. From within its folds she withdrew a stubby white candle and a Zippo. She lit the wick, carefully shielding the flame from the breeze, and handed the candle to Jeff.

She said, "Here is a candle to light you to bed; and here is a chopper to chop off your head!" I screamed and ducked behind Jeff, who calmed her with tranquil murmurs of assent as he shoved her out of the apartment. But the claw remained fast in the doorway.

"You owe me four hundred dollars," she rasped, spittle flying. "Can we make an arrangement?"

"Yes, yes!" he shouted, heaving the door against her.

"Jeff, you're going to break her!" I cried, peeking over his meaty shoulder.

The hag gave the door a mighty shove and stared as though seeing me for the first time. She gasped, "*Who* are you?"

I gulped. "His woman?"

Jeff took advantage of her surprise and slammed the door shut. She hummed a funeral dirge as she drifted down the fire escape.

He blew out the candle and tossed it in a bucket under the Peg-Board. It landed on a pile of a hundred others. He clapped his hands together, rubbed them, and said brightly, "Well! Shall we begin?"

I stumbled wearily to the futon. "I can't even remember why I'm here," I said. "What was that thing?"

He dismissed the whole episode with a wave of his hand. "Just the landlady. Annoying monthly drama."

I spread out some relatively clean newspaper on the futon and sat down. "And what about Lynyrd Skynyrd on the front step?" I ignored the mental image of righteous Val defending his favorite mustaches.

Fat Bald Jeff barked that he'd already told me all about these people and that we had better settle down to create our scandalous website. I would have liked to argue, but it was already five minutes past my dinnertime.

It was dark by the time I boarded the lousy California Avenue bus. I was terrifically nervous about walking the three remaining blocks home from the bus stop, so I held my pepper spray out in front of me and loudly sang "Love on the Rocks" with a fervor that would have made Neil Diamond sick with envy.

Made it to the building unmolested. Paco was sitting on the front stoop, smoking Pall Malls. How relieved I am to have Paco on my front stoop instead of a trailer-trash ruffian! Even if his cigarette smoke defiles my bronchial tubes.

"New neighbor," he said, pointing to a U-Haul parked in front. A handsome man emerged from the truck, carrying a box marked CHINA. He smiled and said, "Excuse me" as he passed me on the sidewalk. Thrills! What good luck: he had looks, breeding, manners, and his own china. Quite old, though—he must be forty—but who better to appreciate my youth and charm? And judging by the way he appraised my figure, in spite of the matronly A-line, he couldn't be a member of the fancy lads' club.

Would've helped him carry his belongings upstairs, except my arms have the strength of bendy straws. Went into my bedroom to think about the future, now that Fat Bald Jeff had shown me the promise of our website. Scary to think of Fat Bald Jeff, slaving for ten years in the Hole without a raise, without real friends, without hope. But Jeff said everything had changed for him now. It had taken him almost two years to compile the evidence he had, two years of waiting for the right moment to present it to the public.

"This makes those ten years worthwhile," he said.

"But what about afterward?" I asked. "When it all blows over?"

He smiled grimly. "It will never really blow over for me, because I will have been the one who caught them at their nasty little games. Even if you are the only one who knows that I was behind it."

But his life wouldn't really change just because of a little prank, would it? Mine would remain just as rustic and lacking in financial excess. Our jobs would still be deadening, our bosses still creepy—just more careful about hiding their misdeeds.

"Don't be too sure," he warned.

My bedroom could do with a little change, but I needed money for that. The Lemming had never been very generous about lending money. Felt sad to be stuck in a bedroom painted landlord beige. What I had to show for myself after twenty-six years of struggling against mediocrity: a three-legged dresser with chipped paint; a closet full of thrift-store glamour, just this side of ragged; a ceramic lamp made by Father that shorted out and jolted me every once in a while; a wobbly nightstand that held my drink recipe book and Gran's old Bible. Of everything I owned, the nightstand was probably the nicest item, and *that* used to belong to Val. I covered it with a lace doily, but I could still see pentagrams carved on the surface.

Without Val Wayne, I would be truly alone in this world. Gran is too consumed with her physical ailments to care about me anymore, and Mother is obsessed with ham-fisted Sweno, king of Norway.

When my parents finally turned the minibus toward home after two and a half uncivilized years of peddling and communing, I was fifteen, and they weren't speaking to each other anymore. They enrolled me midsemester in a progressive school in Evanston, a Montessori where we students selected our own topics for study. I said I was interested in dresses and flowers, so they put me in home ec and biology. Val was my lab partner, and when we refused to dissect our frog on moral grounds, the teacher clasped us to her bosom and congratulated us. You cannot rebel at a Montessori!

Val's parents were hopeless hippie idealists too, but at least by the eighties they had decided to get jobs. *My* father was still chanting under the kitchen table and digging in forests for magical roots. Val had been an outcast at our school, where he was not just the only black student, but the only burnout. It was the burnout status that alienated him. The teachers encouraged him to select an African name, to get in touch with his ancestry. He called himself Black Moor for a while, but confided to me that it celebrated not the invasive Barbary Coast Muslims, but rather the mystical Ritchie Blackmore, Deep Purple guitarist. After school, when our classmates went off to sit on the commons and discuss Nietzsche over coffee, Val offered me corn-silk cigarettes, which we smoked behind the jousting arena.

"One day," I had said, "I'm really going to rebel. I'm going to marry a rich old buzzard with plenty of footmen and Aubusson tapestries on the walls."

"One day," he said, drawing out his chained wallet and showing me a creased magazine picture of Duane Allman folded within, "I'm going to have a mustache like this."

Our friendship had been cemented right there. We both longed for things we couldn't possibly have, but neither of us was cruel enough to tell the other.

Even my parents liked him, and said they felt secure about me going off to school at University of Illinois in Champaign-Urbana because Val was going too. Unable to attend a really choice university (Grandmother had *some* money but had wasted most of it on food and rent for my parents), I was relinquished to whatever lousy education she could afford. Aghast at the prospect of a state school and its lack of old money and social connections, I threw myself on the loom during textile workshop day and bawled. Val set aside the druid costume he'd been creating for his final project and comforted me.

"Don't cry, Addie," he'd said. "You might meet some rich kids at U. of I. Sometimes they go to state schools, if they're really stupid."

"They do?" I whimpered.

"Sure. And try not to think of it as a state school, but as a really-far-away-from-your-parents school." That helped. As it turned out, my classmates were not well-connected Old Boys as I had hoped, nor corn-fed bumpkins as I had feared, but just suburban dolts who played Hackey Sack on the quad all day.

When my father died right after graduation, Val helped Mother sort out his things. Aunt Jane was useless, Grandmother was too grief-stricken, and I had to heat up casseroles and launder Gran's hankies.

Val had been boxing up Father's suits to take to Goodwill, and he offered Gran some sympathetic words on his way out. She'd been weeping for days on our sofa, taking breaks only to spike the tea and stare at Father's baptismal picture.

"He's in a better place now, Mrs. Prewitt," said Val.

Gran sat up, dried her eyes, and looked around at our dump of a house. "Yes, dear Val, that's for sure."

So when Val knocked on my bedroom door tonight, I longed to confide in him all the plans Fat Bald Jeff and I had brewing. But Jeff had ordered me to keep my yap shut. I was somewhat offended, as everyone knows I'm no gossip. Heaven knows the only thing I've ever tried to be in my life was a comfort to my parents.

"Your mom called," he said.

"Good Lord, that prying shrew! What does she want?"

"She was upset because she and Jann were breaking up. She said she tried to call you at work, but you were busy," he answered. Mother loves to air her linens.

"Hooray!" I cried. "I can't believe it. Finally something is going my way!"

Val regarded me sternly and said, "Why don't you stop thinking about yourself for five minutes and call her?"

"Oh yes," I said, fairly giggling with glee. "I shall be a most sympathetic ear while she's tossing his barbells and great, striped exercise pants out the window. I can't *believe* my good fortune! First the handsome new neighbor and now this."

Val asked what new neighbor, so I took him out into the hallway to peer down between the banisters at 2R.

"I can only hope 2F is less standoffish with him than they are with me," I said, but Val shushed me as the good-looking gent emerged from the apartment followed by a decrepit elderly lady.

"I think that's it, Mom," he said. "Call if you need anything."

The old horror sneered at him and made a comment about sons who abandon their mothers to live in slums.

"Okay, Mom," he said mechanically. "See you soon." And he left.

Val and I exchanged puzzled glances. It couldn't be! There was a perfectly good nursing home only a block away. She couldn't be living *here* with us, the bright young things, not counting Paco and the giantess and the lonely drifter in 1R.

The lady looked up through the banisters at us. "Who's there?" she croaked.

"Just your neighbors in 3R," called out Val. She narrowed her already-slitty eyes, appraising us. I bet she was one of those Hungarians; they're always appraising others through distrustful, narrowed eyes.

"Living in sin, are you?" she said and disappeared inside her apartment. We heard all the locks turn, then the sound of something heavy being dragged across the floor and shoved against her door.

"I can't believe it," I said, drinking warm milk and whiskey out of the FIFTY AND FOXY mug. "Why is this happening to me? You know I can't abide old people."

"I can't believe she thinks I would live in sin with someone who looks like Austin Powers."

I said, "Forget about blasting Uriah Heep and Deep Purple anymore." He groaned and dropped his head into his hands. "And no more drinking in the laundry room," I despaired. "Or the hallways or the backyard."

"No more dragging your drunk ass up the stairs," he said. "And she'll completely freak out when she sees Stefan and Mr. Chung making out by the mailboxes like they do when Grandma Chung sends her biweekly check."

Depressed as I was, the only thing that would cheer me up now would be hearing Mother's tearful rendition of Jann's desertion.

"I wonder why she wants to talk to *me*?" I mused.

Val said, "Who else is she going to call? Your grandmother? *She* takes more delight in your mom's misfortunes than you do."

Dialed her up. Val's wrong, you know. I take delight in her *good* fortune, which is getting rid of that lumbering Swede.

Mother said Jann went back to his mama's house, and she had called there repeatedly to no avail. Jann's mama just says he's sitting in their smokehouse, watching the chubs cure.

"Well, Mother, some men cannot break the old apron strings. They can't commit to any woman while Mama is still around," I said.

"That's not it," she sobbed. "He wanted to get married, but I said I wasn't ready."

You could have knocked me over with white-plumed pampas grass!

She continued, "He started thinking about it after I made that comment in the car about one day being her new daughter-in-law. I was just making a joke, but he's obsessed with the idea. And now I've broken his heart and he's left me."

This was much worse than I'd suspected! "Mother, you must move immediately and leave no forwarding address. Change your phone number. Find some type of squat on the West Side to hole up in until he has completely forgotten you! Now, now!"

She blew her nose into the receiver and nearly knocked my eardrum out. "I don't know, Ad. I can't go back to squatting. I'd gotten used to tailgating Bears games and Rollerblading with Jann in Grant Park."

"Mother! He's just trying to force you into subservience. All he wants is a maid and a cook and a whore!"

She sounded puzzled. "Jann? No, I don't think so. He's a wonderful man, any woman would be proud to be his wife. He made the best smoked chubs and taught me to repair the leaky faucet. Your father didn't like fixing things; he said it interfered with the natural order."

I brought out the cannon. "You can stay here with Val and me. I'll tell Jann you joined a convent in Cicero."

She sounded sadder than ever. "I can't believe he won't see me. I don't know if I could be married again, but how can I go on without him? We were going to take kickboxing lessons together. *Maybe* I could be a good wife. God knows it would be a lot easier this time, without children consuming every last . . . well, I mean—"

"Yes," I replied coldly, "I quite understand." Hung up and brooded over her words.

Val came in later, after I had changed into my white cotton nightgown with the blue daisies and frilly hem and settled down in bed. I took the Bible out of the nightstand drawer, searching out the comforting phrases about bad women sentenced to burn in fiery torment.

"Want to talk about it?"

I shook my head.

He looked at the Bible in my hands. "Thought you didn't believe in God anymore," he said.

"Of course I do. *Someone's* got to make my mother pay."

He parted the curtains on my window, letting in a veil of sodium light, and looked out across the gangway. "Ever hear that little dog cry over there? It's driving me up the goddamn wall."

My spirits were lifted at work when Jeff stopped me in the dungeon at the coffee counter and whispered that stage one of our plan would be going into effect tonight.

I whispered back, "How can we make sure everyone will see the website right away?"

He said he'd rigged up a way to send anonymous global e-mail messages throughout the building and that the first one alerting the staff to the site would go out tomorrow morning at nine.

"You need to have it written before you leave tonight, though," he added.

"Me?" I squeaked. "*You* write it! Why do I have to?"

"Frankly," said Fat Bald Jeff, "you have a talent for poison-pen letters that I have not."

"What are you talking about?"

He said, "The letters to the CTA supposedly from Coddles."

I gasped, looking around furtively. "How did you know? I never saved them on the computer."

He smiled and lifted his shoulders modestly. "It's cute how reckless nontech staff are about private electronic documents. Oh, don't worry, I won't tell anyone. But can I count on you to write the introductory e-mail?"

Thought about it. Why not? Life was already a shambles, and my future—as neighbor to a suffocating old person and stepdaughter to a hulking Nordic bricklayer—rose before me like a black sun on the horizon. "Yes, you can. As they say, the only thing we have to lose is our change."

He sighed. "It's *chains*, Addie."

"Oh. That makes sense. Although it's so annoying, my handbag is always loaded down with pennies—" He just waved away my words and stumped back into the Hole.

Took the elevator back up to the second floor. They should have a bench in there. It's tiring, standing all that time. Back in the cube, I found myself growing more excited about our plan. Felt like a renegade Robin Hood, stealing embarrassing info from the powerful. And with it, maybe we could help some poor zombies, or whatever.

I had been poking around in the photo archives and found a picture of Bev, Coddles, and Mr. Genett stuffing themselves at the Christmas party buffet as Big Lou, the erstwhile janitor, cleaned up the mess they left on the floor. Big Lou was fired shortly thereafter when the operations manager found company squeegees in Lou's locker—according to Jeff, the OM planted them there after Big Lou found the OM feeling up the personnel director (a crotchety sea-hag) in the maintenance closet. Jeff agreed that the party photo could go on the splash page of the website; he wanted to use the caption PIGS AT THE TROUGH — WE'VE HAD ENOUGH! I'd pointed out that "trough" didn't rhyme with "enough," but he said if William Blake could rhyme "eye" with "symmetry," then we, too, are allowed some poetic license. I was surprised and impressed that Fat Bald Jeff read anything besides Libertarian propaganda and *Star Trek* pulp. In a merry mood, I shipped another journal off to the printer without proofreading the galleys once!

Have never experienced anything like this at the Place before. Perhaps I've found a new role for myself at work, helping the downtrodden. Our world is a harsh one; nobody knows this better than I.

At 12:05 I stepped into the staff lounge to retrieve my lunch bag. The graphic designers were sitting around the conference table outside the lounge, gorging themselves on bacon cheeseburgers. I looked disapprovingly at Francis. It's disgusting that a boy concerned with the fate of cabdrivers in suspicious circumstances should so ill-use his gastrointestinal tract.

I sat at the table with them, though. Now that I am the publisher of the common man's scandal sheet, I feel I should try to fit into their culture. Francis made room for me, but the delinquents barely gave me an inch. I believe the unenlightened also resisted Saint Benedict as he tried to raise them from their filth.

"I've been thinking over our discussion about Mumia," I said, "and I've come to the conclusion that he is innocent and a victim of our corrupt police system." I stole a sidelong glance at the others, who regarded me with superior skepticism.

"Excellent!" said Francis. "There's a meeting at the anarchists' collective in my neighborhood next week—"

"Well, now," I interrupted, "no need to rush into anything. You've swayed me. Can't I just wear a protest T-shirt under my sweater or something?"

The other boys snickered and got up from the conference table. Francis said that was true; we'd just start off slow and see where things went. I smiled brightly, but in truth I have no intention of entering a filthy anarchists' den and carving aphorisms into my chest. After lunch, I saw Francis rooting around in the supply closet. I asked what he was doing, but he shushed me and glanced slyly over both shoulders.

He whispered, "I'm stealing sticker paper so I can make copies of these." He showed me a manila folder with lots of stickers in it. Each had a slogan of some kind on it, like FREE LEONARD PELTIER or REMEMBER FRED HAMPTON, SENIOR, or BONGS NOT BOMBS.

"I thought you said it was Fred Junior" I commented.

"Junior's in jail, serving eighteen years on a trumped-up arson charge. Senior was murdered by the cops in the middle of the night in the infamous Chicago Panther House Raid," he said. "Don't you know anything about Chicago history?"

"I know when the Saint Valentine's Day massacre was: February fourteenth," I said proudly.

"What year?"

Moved along quickly to another topic. One year is much like another in our city's history of oppression.

"I'll help you copy these," I said.

"You?" he marveled. "Help a graphic delinquent steal office supplies to make political statements?"

I had no answer. All I knew was I felt bad for Big Lou, his name besmirched by planted evidence, and it made me reconsider my judgment of these incarcerated fellows. Even though I have no idea what I'd say to Mumia over tofurkey-havarti sandwiches, I guess we're all sort of humans here together.

We stole some sticker paper out of the supply closet and made many copies of his slogans. He asked if I would like one. The one that appealed to me most had a simple elegance about it: just a white background with black type that read FREE MUMIA.

"But Mumia is only one man—I mean, of course I support the principle, but his case could be settled any minute . . ." I certainly didn't want to be stuck making a passé political statement.

Francis stared at me with cold censure. He informed me that Mumia was a symbol as well as an individual and that his name would always inspire revolution in people and motivate them to fight for the rights of all political prisoners. I must say, Francis's new assertiveness was unexpected—even a little thrilling! Perhaps one day, if our website was ever exposed, people would associate Fat Bald Jeff with insurgence and workingman bravado, instead of techie geekishness and angina.

"And BONGS NOT BOMBS?" I asked. "What is that a symbol of?"

He smiled sheepishly. "That's a personal crusade."

I took a BONGS NOT BOMBS sticker for Val.

Together we posted my new sticker on the nameplate outside my cubicle. Felt very revolutionary. No one could say that I was afraid to voice my opinion on cabdrivers in suspicious circumstances.

By day's end I had finished my e-mail message for Fat Bald Jeff and delivered it in code. Planned to leave at four-thirty since the day was warm and Val and 2F were going to be working in the garden this evening. Peeked down the corridors in case Coddles was prowling about, then tiptoed down the hall. Wait, what was that bit of scribbling near my FREE MUMIA sign? I went back and looked closely. Someone had scrawled—in the coarse illegibility of the criminally insane— the words WITH EVERY PURCHASE below my slogan! I like being a rabble-rouser, but I hate working with the common man.

Chapter 8

TO: All NAL staff
FROM: Crook-Eye, Ltd.
RE: The disgusting truth

[Note to zombie staff: please enjoy the following open letter to the NAL power brokers]

Dear Petty Dullard:
Who said the revolution will not be televised? Let us rephrase that: we transmit the incriminating information; the revolution is up to the people.

Perhaps you ought to start by sequestering yourself in a safe environment. Who knows how your underlings will react when they discover that you—oh, well. Why spoil the fun of letting you find out for yourself? You must have *some* idea . . . right now, in fact, thoughts are racing through your brain: *Has someone found out my secret? Copies of my corporate credit card statements? Kiddie-porn sites bookmarked on my office computer? My dalliance with married coworkers on the floor of the staff cafeteria?* Just keep in mind that videoconferencing cameras come in very handy, and are quite easy to control from remote, untraceable locations.

Your peccadilloes would be comical if they weren't so sickening. We believe in intellectual freedom and equal access to information, so please accept our invitation to browse at your leisure our new website: www.crook-eye.org. After all, everyone should see him- or herself in print—or digital imaging—at least once! The Information Age will indeed be a profitable one—for some of us.

> Sincerely yours,
> Jesus Maria
> Crook-Eye, Ltd., project manager

Had we known just what effect our introductory e-mail and website would have on the National Association of Libraries that fateful morning, we could have set up cameras to record for posterity the massive freak-out that occurred at exactly nine o'clock. There was much wailing and gnashing of teeth in the corridors! Fat Bald Jeff programmed his home computer to send out my global e-mail to all staff first thing in the morn- ing, and as two hundred frantic zombies simultaneously tried to access the Internet, the entire system network crashed. Busy techies struggled for hours to get things up and running again. I played solitaire with a real deck of cards at my desk. It's awfully slow that way, but easier to cheat.

Coddles locked himself in his office shortly after the morning's announcement. I don't blame him. No one respects the authority of middle-management infantilists. Mr. Genett stormed around the halls, knocking bank art off the walls and fuming. Perhaps he shouldn't have redecorated the execu- tive bathroom in favor of purchasing proper equipment for our department! Jeff and I listed that offense on a page titled "Let Them Eat Cake," along with other luxury items bought by the executives on staff budgets. Never really felt akin to the personnel peons before I found out their department head spent three hundred dollars of their weekly budget on fancy coffee for a personal percolator and floral bouquets for her office suite and private bathroom. This forced the personnel peons to use obsolete software and monochrome computer monitors. Also in that section was a transcript of a personal long-distance phone conversation held by the finance director the same day he announced that staff would no longer be able to make personal calls from work, due to budget cuts.

"Administration 101," culled from pirated e-mails that Jeff had routed to his home computer, listed the various unpaid assignments that bosses now expected from their secretaries and assistants, including: buying presents for girlfriends; lying to irate wives on the phone; ordering food; misting plants; and picking up dry cleaning, schoolchildren, expensive coffee, and small dogs from groomers. Only a photograph could adequately explain Miss Fernquist's gross duties to Coddles. Good thing Coddles was too dumb to know how his videoconferencing camera worked, or that Jeff had been able to rig it up through closed circuitry, record the antics on Coddles's desk, and transmit them to the hovel computer via MPEG format for subsequent review.

Lura and Bev came into my cubicle and gossiped about the website for ages, wondering who put it up.

"I don't see why I had to be included in that first picture," complained Bev. "I'm just a copyeditor, not management. And what's with 'Pigs at the Trough'? I was just eating a Christmas party snack like everyone else. Why should I be singled out?"

Because you're a greedy, vile sow, and you've always been mean to me.

Lura said, "They probably just wanted to show Mr. Genett and the other managers scarfing food while the janitor cleaned up after them, and you happened to be in the shot."

Bev said, "I heard from Lynn, the accounting receptionist, that the fourth-floor department head is lining up people outside his office to be interrogated. The brass is determined to find out who's behind the website."

"You don't think they'll do that on our floor, do you?" I asked. This could be a problem. I cannot hold up under fierce inquisition.

Lura stepped back into the hallway and looked both ways. "I don't think so. Mr. Genett is standing outside Coddles's office with the maintenance guys right now, holding a blow torch." We gophered around the side of my cubicle and watched them melt the lock. When they threw open the door, Mr. Genett bellowed, "Albert! Come out from under your desk!" and stalked into the office. We could hear Coddles weeping.

"I can't believe he's crying," I said.

"He got caught buying a blowup doll on the company credit card!" retorted Bev. "There's digital pictures of Fernquist diapering him on his desk! Why shouldn't he cry?"

Lura said dryly, "The bigwigs always cry when they get caught." Just like television evangelists!

We listened to Mr. Genett tear into our blubbering supervisor, shouting, "You've disgraced our department!"

Coddles continued to cry. "Why don't you find out who's responsible for this horrible thing? Maybe it's one of our own staff."

Mr. Genett said, "Please. Who in your unit is bright enough to come up with this? Those punks in graphic design or the lazy girls in editorial? Our gutless salesmen? Production? The production people get lost in the back stairwell."

Coddles cried, "Well, it's probably *them*!"

"We're not lazy," whispered Lura angrily. I was aghast that Bev was lumped into the girl category with Lura and me. He can't possibly think we three are from the same generation.

When Mr. Genett emerged from Coddles's office, the entire department had gathered in the hallway to listen to the fight. No one said anything as Mr. Genett waded through the crowd. He knew we had heard his insults.

Before Mr. Genett reached his office, he turned and screamed at us to get back to work. Everyone made vague movements toward their cubicles, and Mr. Genett went into his office and slammed the door. One of the graphic designers gestured rudely at the closed door, and a lone salesman applauded.

Felt as though I was part of a revolution, if only covertly, and was glad I had worn my red silk scarf today. Wanted to brag about my involvement with the website but remembered I had no friends. My coworkers one by one drifted back into their cubes.

Francis noticed the defaced Mumia Abu-Jamal sticker and came into my cubicle to offer me a replacement, but we couldn't get the old one off my nameplate.

I grunted with the effort of scratching at the edges with my thumbnail.

"Why do they have to be so permanent?"

"Because they're stickers," he said.

We ended up just putting the new one over it. Francis slapped the sticker on sloppily and covered up part of my name. Now the nameplate reads FREE MUMIA DIE PREWITT.

"Sorry," he said.

One of the graphic designers walked by and whinnied, "Where's *my* free Mumia?"

"Graphic delinquent," I said under my breath, but Francis heard me and clucked his tongue in disapproval.

"I mean artist," I said. Old habits die hard.

He said, "It *is* art, you know. It may only be for the cover of a technical library journal or brochure about the staff carnival, but I try to pick cool graphics and clean fonts. I'm no Gauguin, but this year's Hot Dog Day flyer was killer."

"I'm all for art," I insisted. "And I'm glad you're no Gauguin. I don't really care for mustardy paintings of native women."

"Listen," he said, "what do you think of that website? I think it's really great, especially how that one article listed the similarities between the canning of Big Lou in maintenance and the conviction of Mumia Abu-Jamal."

I turned back to my desk and shuffled my deck of cards nervously. "Yes, it appears Mumia has made it into the public consciousness."

Francis stroked his stubble and said, "Has he?"

After lunch, the network collapsed again, and I was forced to copyedit drivel on paper. Took my time with seventeen pencils at the pencil sharpener in the common area and overheard gossip to the effect that certain of our production slaves were thought to be responsible for the Crook-Eye website. The production slaves! The hoi-polloi can hardly *read,* let alone compose poisonous prose! I was disgusted.

"Well, I heard it was that one security guard who was fired last year for constantly looking over the stalls in the sixth-floor women's bathroom," said one secretary.

"But Coddles thinks it was the production people," objected another.

The third secretary whispered conspiratorially to the others, "Whenever anything goes wrong around here, it's always the temp's fault." They all looked over at the temp in the middle of the room, who was asleep at his desk.

The third secretary stepped toward the temp, delicately sniffing the air. Spite withered her pointy bird face.

She said, "That temp really stinks," and pulled a can of Lysol out of the supply closet. She sprayed a big cloud over him. He coughed a little in his sleep.

The secretaries saw me lollygagging at the pencil sharpener and stared at me until I left.

There was no point in editing anything else, as the network kept crashing and zombies kept distracting me. They congregated in the hallways, talking about the website and speculating on the perpetrators. Four-thirty could not come soon enough. Last evening, Val and 2F had finally issued me a decent invitation to join in on the garden. I must have drifted around the yard for half an hour, staring forlornly into the manure pile, before they relented and asked me to participate. Val gave me the good news as 2F smirked in the background. I found their smugness incomprehensible, but then I have resigned myself to being the ignorant third wheel in their little group.

"You mean fifth wheel," Val said. "The third wheel is an integral part of any automobile." We were all going to run up to a nearby nursery, owned by Chung's brother, for some plants tonight. Scandal sheets and cold-hardy perennials—now this is living! I might even call Mother and try to be sympathetic again. As a daughter, I pride myself on being a great comfort in rough times.

On my way out of the building (front door this time), I passed Fat Bald Jeff waiting for the elevator. He had just run out to the Italian joint next door and bought himself armloads of biscotti. I guess he was throwing over yucko vending-machine horror Bun in favor of exciting European pastry! Only *I* knew his fantastic expenditure was in celebration of our scheme. As I walked by, he shifted his weight from one fat foot to the other, scowled, slowly shut one eye, then opened it. Ah, a small signal in a code among spies, but it meant success. None of the zombies milling about the lobby would have guessed our clandestine partnership, nor would they have interpreted the grimacing wink as anything more than acid reflux or lazy eye.

In keeping with the secret signs, I said, "The biscotti look good today."

He furrowed his brow and said, "I guess."

I implored him with my eyes. "The baking of the biscotti seems to have gone well, wouldn't you say?"

He inhaled deeply and nodded, flaring his nostrils and fluttering his eyelids. Come on, Jeff, now is not the time to play the fat, bald coquette.

I pressed on. "The oven was hot, no?"

The doors opened and he stepped into the elevator. "Yes, I get it."

"But—" I sputtered as the doors began to close.

He smiled as he shoved three biscotti into his mouth. "There'll be more."

I looked around in alarm—had anyone eavesdropped? —but the only person in hearing distance was Earl, the un-armed desk official, and he was snoring in his chair. On the front of the reception desk, someone had slapped a BONGS NOT BOMBS sticker.

Didn't have time to muse over Jeff's cryptic "more." Got back to the building shortly after five. Val was not home yet, and Paco and 2F were standing around the garden plots, talking vegetables.

"Peppers, eggplant, tomatoes." Paco ticked off the list on his gnarled fingers.

"Right," said Chung, marking off his clipboard with a Sharpie.

I spoke up. "I'd like a few varieties of radicchio, for my sliced tofurkey tarragon sandwiches."

Everyone looked at me blankly. Chung shrugged and made a tiny mark on the clipboard.

Stefan stepped forward and regarded me for a moment. He seemed to be sizing me up for some task. The blond comma of hair fell attractively over one icy eye, and he folded his arms across his chest.

"We're all going to have jobs here in the garden," he began. "Paco has volunteered to water the perennials and vegetables and prune shrubbery. Val will be cutting the grass and weeding the side bed. I will be coordinating the purchase and application of manure and organic fertilizer and pesticides. Chung here will oversee plant and color selection and will haggle skillfully with his cheap brother about the prices. Your job is to weed the vegetable bed and to assist Alma, who is too infirm and crotchety to plant and take care of her vegetables."

Alma? The Hungarian wretch in 2R! No wonder 2F looked so satisfied when I accepted their gardening invitation. I *am* the fifth wheel.

"If the old woman can't tend her own plants, then she shouldn't get involved," I protested. "Who asked her, anyway?"

"Oh, that's nice," said Stefan, "deny an elderly lady some vegetables in her twilight years. Very generous of you." I saw three pairs of eyebrows descend in disapproval and three mouths harden into censorious frowns. Chung began to draw a line through my name on the clipboard.

"No, wait, I'll do it," I replied hurriedly. "But why me?"

"The rest of us already have jobs. Take it or leave it."

I swallowed glumly and nodded, looking up at the back porch off 2R. The decrepit witch stood there, a grim line of satisfaction cutting across her shriveled apple head.

She called down, "Hop to it, young woman. I gave the Chinaman a list of things I want."

Mr. Chung muttered something exotic and violent under his breath and handed me her list. Chinaman! It's obvious to anyone he is Korean.

When Val got home from work, we all piled into Paco's station wagon and drove off. Stefan sat in the front seat, and

Val and Chung sat in the back. When I slid in next to them, Chung said he needed to sit cross-legged or he'd get carsick, and would I mind sitting in the way back? I heard distinct giggling as I clambered into the space usually reserved for dogs and fifth wheels. My khaki gardening skirt was not engineered for gymnastics.

"Maybe you should have worn jeans," said Val.

I tightened the babushka around my head and vowed to ignore them the rest of the ride.

After selecting Alma's ridiculous vegetables and seeds—what kind of lunatic chooses watercress over arugula?—I was at last free to wander about the perennials and choose a few for myself. The men were not big on flowers, except for Paco's boring marigolds and 2F's hideous hybrid tea roses. Alma's puckered, aged face loomed before me, and I found myself picking poisonous plants.

"Monkshood?" questioned Mr. Chung's brother, looking down at the quart container on my little red wagon. "Be careful. Every part of that plant is lethal." Its bell-shaped blue flowers would look pretty lightly brushing against Alma's insipid mustard greens.

When we got home (again I was relegated to the way back of the station wagon, thorny rose canes jabbing me on all sides), we set out our plants in the garden, rearranging them for effect as Chung calculated space for seeds. I was dead tired and longed to rest, but I am not the type of girl who sits in the dirt. Laid across the picnic table and fell asleep.

Val jabbed me awake with the trowel. He said more work could be done tomorrow. I hopped off the picnic table and fell down. The fancy lads' club had tied my shoelaces together!

We walked up the stairs with 2F and said good-bye. They reminded Val about going barware shopping with them this weekend, in preparation for next month's blowout. I stood by expectantly, awaiting my party invitation.

"Well, good-night," they sang gaily, then shut the blasted door.

Fumed up the next flight, but turned when I heard their door open a crack.

Stefan called out, "Val, invite that hot, dark-haired guy who hoisted your roommate up the stairs the other night, will you?" Then giggling broke out behind the door as it clicked shut.

"Oh, come on." Val sighed as I threw a modest tantrum in the hallway. He pushed me toward the door, and before impact I caught sight of myself in our highly polished door knocker. Someone had drawn half a mustache on me with permanent marker.

Skipped work. Spent forty minutes scrubbing my upper lip this morning as Val pretended not to notice. We ate our cereals in silence as our eyes drifted involuntarily to the other's half 'stache.

"It wasn't me," he finally said, picked up his keys, and ran out the door.

Scrounged around in the back of my closet and dragged out Mother's filthy old sari. I'd used it previously for a Halloween costume; today it would function as clothing. Luckily it had flecks of red running throughout the fabric, so I tied my red silk scarf across the lower half of my face and left the apartment. Only one person could make me feel better.

"Girl!" A thin, reedy voice called out as I fled down the stairs. "Girl! You come by later so we can plan my vegetable patch."

"Thrills!" I shouted back and left the building.

Sitting and smoking on the front stoop was Jadwiga, the building janitoress. She smirked at me as I adjusted my face scarf.

"Hadn't you better clean something?" I snapped.

She appraised my grotesque, bedraggled sari and said, "Hadn't *you*?"

How dare the cleaning woman speak to me in that tone! Made a mental note to write a letter of complaint to the landlord. Walked briskly to the El. It was a bit nippy out, so I had to wear the fake Burberry over my sari. Looked asinine, but as my world is collapsing under the weight of Alma and my disfigurement, I really do not care. Crook-Eye, Ltd., is the only thing that keeps me going.

Called Fat Bald Jeff at work from the train station. He answered on the twelfth ring.

"Tech support," he droned into the phone.

"Are the biscotti fresh today?"

Silence. Then, "Where are you? I went up to your cubicle, but Bev said you were playing hooky."

"I'm not playing hooky! I have a slight physical ailment."

"Please," he interrupted, "no more about your spastic colon."

It's not spastic colon. It's irritable bowel, as I must have told him a thousand times.

He asked me to meet him at his hovel tonight. He said the biscotti were in a fantastic uproar in the oven and we needed a new recipe.

Hung up the phone and a unique sensation crept over me. Could it be the satisfaction of a job well done?

Train seemed to travel faster than usual, and no one asked me for change in my stinking getup. When I exited in Evanston, the sun was shining and tulips were blooming everywhere. Stripped off the wretched raincoat and let the sun beat down on my sari. Walked down the quaint Main Street and caught my reflection in a bookshop window. Minus the Ernie Douglas spectacles and protruding bucks beneath the face scarf, I made a terrifically fetching foreigner.

Gran was heartily surprised to see me, though a look of horror crossed her face as she took in the sari. Scandalous memories of Mother must have come flooding back. I lifted the face scarf, revealed the mustache, and told the whole story.

"Oh!" she said, relieved. "But I don't think Indian women cover their faces. It's the Arabs."

I am not about to drape myself in a hideous black shroud just to look authentic. The sari is bad enough, but at least it is short-sleeved and cinched about the waist. I look awful in drab colors and shapeless muumuu things.

Gran shuffled around looking for an ointment that would remove the mustache. I relaxed in her chintzy overstuffed armchair. Calmly regarding me from the wall of framed pictures was Father, age twenty.

I didn't care for that smug smile across the room. So I'm wearing Mother's repulsive sari, so what? I had to, to complement my red silk face scarf.

Gran came back with a foul-smelling unguent, which she smeared across my upper lip. The stench and the complacent grin of Father reminded me of the goat-salve incident of my childhood.

"When Harvey was a young man, I used this cream on him that time he carved your mother's and his initials in his arm, interwoven with crudely drawn roses," she said. "Why did he have to use his left hand? We never *could* get rid of that scar."

I remembered the ugly deformity on his bicep. Have hated roses ever since. Why not the subtle prairie gentian? Why scarification at all? I would never carve the Lemming's initials in my flesh. It's bad enough that he leaves thumbprints on our doorknobs.

"There," she said, sitting back to survey her work. "Just let it sit."

She didn't ask why there was half a mustache drawn on me with a Sharpie, or why I came all the way out to Evanston just for smelly salve. She picked up the newspaper and worked on the crossword puzzle, pausing only to ask about five-letter rumba bandleaders and six-letter Hungarian sheepdogs.

On the wall behind her, near the fireplace, was a wooden rack of Delft china. Photos in sterling frames hung over the couch—me in my christening dress with my parents standing gloomily in the background, Father dressed in a Nehru jacket and Mother in her sari; Gran and Grandfather posing by a newly planted buckeye tree with teenage Father asleep in the hammock; my parents' wedding day, such as it was, with Reverend Rainbow Dog officiating; vacationing at the seaside in Truro, Massachusetts, with grandparents and parents, everyone sitting in the sand and smiling.

"Gran? Sometimes I think if Father were around now, he might like the direction my life is heading."

She smiled, not really understanding what I meant, of course. "Well, Adelaide, dear, he had some strange ways, but he always said he loved his little princess more than life itself."

"Me?" I asked. "I'm the princess?"

"Of course."

"That was the word he used, 'princess'? Not 'Prissy Princess,' but just plain 'princess'?"

She nodded. Wow. I *always* wanted to be a princess.

Grandmother said her head hurt, and she put down the newspaper and stared out the window, chin resting in the palm of her hand. My eyes filled up with tears, due to the pungency of the ointment.

All that remained of the mustache was a red blotch of irritation. Changed out of the lousy sari into pedal pushers and pink cotton blouse and tramped downstairs to Alma's.

"Sit down, girl," she commanded. I obeyed, after slipping a magazine between me and her mildewy couch. Alma wore a buffalo-plaid men's shirt with a tweed skirt and old-lady brogues. Her hair was an untidy mound of salt-and-pepper curls. Her apartment was stuffed with romance paperbacks, squalid rugs, cruddo furniture, ashtrays, and unpacked boxes. A tabby cat sat on the windowsill, licking itself silly. Alma lit a cigarette and eyeballed me. I coughed.

"Been necking, I see," she said.

As if! Anyone who has applied more than udder balm to one's face in the past fifty years could see that my lip was swollen and red from cosmetic treatment, not necking. I began to explain but she cut me off.

"Never mind," she said. "You girls are loose these days. Can't expect better. Anyway, I've come up with a new list of chores for you. Get cracking."

I grabbed the list. Nestled among the mundane garden tasks were orders to sweep her porch, take out her garbage, and empty the cat box.

This is the thanks I get for being a kind and unselfish person! I said I couldn't touch the cat box as I am allergic. She squinted at me, but I kept my eyes wide and honest. As for the garbage, we agreed that if she left it bagged properly in the hall, I'd take it to the Dumpster on my way to work. I'd sweep her stinking back porch once a week, as long as I didn't have to walk through her apartment to get there. I'd take my chances on the rickety fire escape.

"What's that noise?" she asked suddenly.

I explained about the white puppy in the cage next door. We went to her second bedroom (in it stood an army cot and piles of horrible clothes) and looked out the window. Alma said, "Poor bastard," while I counted the number of cigarette holes in her shirt (twelve).

Then she showed me pictures of her children and called them filthy names.

"A child that abandons his mother is worse than the devil himself," said Alma. "I suppose you've left your mother alone in some nursing home somewhere."

I looked at her in shock. She couldn't possibly think I am old enough to have a rest-home inmate for a parent. I replied that my mother is not even fifty and lives in sin with a bricklayer. Alma nearly choked on her Lucky Strike.

"Oh, I almost forgot," I said. "I brought you a little present."

Astonished, she took the package that I had brought down with me. She cleared her throat a few times and said, "Hmph. *Ten Little Indians.* I never cared much for mysteries. But thanks."

"You'll like this one," I said. "It has a surprise ending."

Escaped back to my apartment in time for dinner. Soothed myself with leftover Waldorf salad and Val's old ginger brandy. He came home from work and zeroed in on my upper lip. Relief softened his expression, but he said nothing. I gave him the BONGS NOT BOMBS sticker, kind of a peace treaty. He was really happy and mounted it on his driftwood Jesus clock.

"Something smells funny," he said, poking around the garbage.

"It's me," I said matter-of-factly. "I stink from the ink-removing ointment."

He nodded seriously. Then he paused, moved closer to me, and sniffed the air again. "No. It's something else. You smell like an old person."

Ick. "Oh. I was in Alma's apartment."

"God, it stinks to be old," he said. I laughed lamely at his pun. Senior bashing seemed unfunny today.

He looked at me. "Are you going to shower?"

Of course not. I had to go to Fat Bald Jeff's.

* * *

Endured the nightmare bicycle ride to the hovel. Wore Val's motorcycle helmet from his *Wild One* phase. I have no bike helmet, and the rain bonnet really offers no protection from today's moronic drivers. Crept down Jeff's sidewalk. It seemed the grotesque mongrel in the front yard had stretched its chain, and I could feel its spittle and mangy whiskers as it tried to savage me.

"Stay," I ordered. It advanced. "No," I ordered again, with more force this time. It growled, shook its muzzle, and flecked me with bubbling foam.

If only Francis were here! He's one of those animal rights fanatics and would know what to do. As a great lover of animals (except sordid housecats that lick themselves), I managed to feel sorry for the dog even as I planned to squash it beneath my nine-hundred-pound bike. Unfortunately, I lifted the bicycle only a few inches off the ground before I dropped it squarely on my false Chanel ballet flats.

"Shit!" I screamed, howling in anguish.

The mongrel promptly relieved itself on my bicycle and ran headfirst into the plastic garden gnome.

Left the bike outside, unlocked, and ran trembling up Jeff's fire escape. Worse than the near-brutal attack upon my person and bike was the vision of Jeff's wraith of a landlady slithering out his window and dropping down on bare, fungal feet to the fire escape. She smiled absently at me, patted her fright wig, and descended the steps.

Rushed past Fat Bald Jeff into the safety of the hovel. He agreed that the mongrel must have been put on a longer chain, as it had taken a nip at his nether regions after work today. It was pure providence that Jeff's wallet, stuffed with five years' worth of receipts and forty-five coupons for Ron's Pizza and Chicken George, protected his backside from the snapping jaws. What's worse, he said, was that the landlady's son (the trailer-trash philistine) had cornered him by the garbage cans last night and threatened him with bodily harm unless Jeff returned the purloined pot.

"You can tell me, Jeff," I said. "Did you steal his marijuana?"

A purple vein stood out on his forehead and his eyeballs vibrated within their sockets. Through clenched, ground-down teeth he said, "Do I seem like I smoke a lot of pot?"

I suggested that maybe he ought to start. He merely popped the top off a root beer Fanta and, without taking his eyes from me, slogged it all in one swig. A little dribbled down his chin, but I dared not say a thing.

He shoved a can of grape Fanta at me, which I reluctantly sipped after a thorough rubdown with my hanky. Couldn't help but ask what he was doing with the landlady in his apartment.

"She broke in through the window," he retorted. "I didn't let her in. I was busy polishing my samurai swords in the bathtub." I looked over at the creepo metal tub. Swords were strewn about on the floor and toilet, drying on towels.

"Anyway," he continued, "I'm a month behind on the rent and she came up to collect. So I agreed to have dinner with her next week so we could discuss the payment arrangement." He shuddered.

"Do you mean you'd submit to a battery of corpse kisses and fondling just to offset your rent?" I asked in disbelief.

Fat Bald Jeff narrowed his eyes at me. I gulped some Fanta and looked away. He knows a bit too much about my financial aspirations with the Lemming.

He said, "I have no choice. I was bypassed for another raise, and she wants to jack up the rent an additional twenty-five bucks. She says the neighborhood is in transition and she wants to be on top of the gentrification wave." Mrs. Nibbett, though completely mad, is a shrewd capitalist.

He sat down at his computer and motioned for me to pull up a dilapidated hassock. It was warm up in the attic, even though it was not yet May. At the rear, there was a round window the size of a basketball and some holes in the roof where pigeons flew in to roost. I said summer must be brutal up here, but he just shrugged and said in the hot months he did most of his work in the bathtub.

As Jeff brought up the website, a smile split his head like a melon. He said there'd been talk in the Hole about organizing a protest rally to get Big Lou rehired. Jeff had finally tracked down a photo he thought he'd lost, of the operations manager skulking about Lou's locker with an armload of squeegees. Hope surged within me, as I felt Big Lou was my pet project.

"Jeff," I said breathlessly, "I feel so weird. It's all tied up with Big Lou being exonerated and our co-zombies getting a good look at what the brass has been up to. I can't explain it . . . it's like, like—"

"Concern for another human being?" he suggested.

It's *possible* that before the advent of Crook-Eye and my education re: the janitorial conspiracy and the larger political prisoner situation, I may have been a mite thoughtless about others.

I asked, "Where did you get all these pictures? The zombies flogging themselves on the dungeon floor during the Christmas party and the OM planting the stolen squeegees and so on?"

Fat Bald Jeff smiled wryly. He said he had a source, another employee even more disgruntled than he. Who could be more disgruntled than Fat Bald Jeff? He wouldn't name anyone, other than to say that guys who've pushed the mail cart around the halls of the Place for thirty years accumulate a lot of information without being seen.

"I thought the mailroom people were all temps," I said. He said that was a common misconception; most employees viewed low-level, invisible peons as temps. Felt humbled. I may have to get used to my views being common.

After a moment I said, "Some people have it worse than I do at the Place."

He patted me kindly on the shoulder and said, "You're learning."

Fat Bald Jeff then recounted the day's reign of disorder. The constant influx of e-mail between staff had shut down the network again. Department heads were demanding action from the top executives, who in turn demanded action from the department heads. Zombies were questioned all day long by their unit heads, and tech support was ordered to search all files on the building network. Many employees placed burning votive candles and bouquets of flowers by Big Lou's old locker. The previous night, Fat Bald Jeff had left anonymous messages at the news desk of the *Chicago Sun-Times*, alerting them to the website. A reporter contacted him before work by a secret e-mail address and conducted a brief online interview about the misdeeds and criminal activities of the bigwigs at the Place. Jeff faxed him copies of his information, and the reporter called the executive director of the Place for her point of view. She had a big fit on the phone, and the first article in a series on corporate crime would appear tonight in the evening edition of the *Sun-Times*!

"Did you tell the reporter you were Jesus Maria, project manager?" I asked.

"Oh no," he replied, "that's yours. I gave my alias as the Ham Sandwich, vice president."

Jeff leaned back in his chair, folded his hands over his big belly, and smiled wickedly. He looked like a dark and demented Friar Tuck.

I said, "This is going to be big, isn't it?"

He said, "Yes."

We updated the site with new pictures and text, including a shot of Coddles crying under his desk while Mr. Genett threatened him. Jeff explained that the videoconferencing camera and the computer in Coddles's office were always on, recording everything digitally, even though Coddles assumed he was turning his computer off at night.

I shook my head. "I still don't really understand how you managed to do this."

Jeff smiled grimly and said, "Closed circuitry. Other stuff. I've been recording this crap for years through the video-conferencing software. On my lunch hour today, I installed a tiny digital camera on the front of my anonymous mailroom contact's mail cart. I think we got some good pictures of zombies outside their supervisors' offices, waiting to be interrogated. I've also been futzing with the accounting mainframe so that it sends my hovel computer duplicates of expenditures on the individual department budgets." He showed me an expense report. It seemed that *every* department head had used surplus budget to redecorate bigwig offices or build executive bathrooms. No one spent money on ergonomic computer chairs. The hump between my shoulder blades throbbed in resentment.

We sat down and designed a new splash page to replace "Pigs at the Trough." As Jeff searched for appropriate graphics, I began with a short Crook-Eye mission statement. I wrote several snarky drafts but settled on the plainest one, the one least snide. Somehow, it expressed my real feelings most clearly.

> Thank you for visiting our home page again. No doubt we piqued your interest yesterday with our brutal, unflinching exposé of the NAL executives. Our purpose in posting this website is not merely to humiliate our bosses, but to incite your outrage at the offensive acts they have committed—heinous crimes that end up robbing us not only of decent work conditions but of our human rights as well. Perhaps they will think twice next time they spend surplus company budget on bank art for their washrooms instead of proper desk chairs for employees. Perhaps they will reconsider propositioning the administrative staff with the promise of salary perks in exchange for vile groping in the cafeteria. Our purpose is to elevate the common laborer, the Big Lous of our world, who have suffered injustices at the claws of the big business behemoth, been sucked dry by the corporate

vampire. Think not-for-profits aren't "corporate" or "big business"? Think again.

Resistance is not futile.

Sincerely,

Jesus Maria and the Ham Sandwich

Fat Bald Jeff read it over in silence. He gruffly threw an arm around my shoulders and squashed me briefly, saying, "Well done." Lump in my throat. Felt like I'd accomplished something worthwhile.

"We should have a logo," he said. "How about a giant bloodshot eyeball to represent us, and a hoe to represent the workers?"

"I have an idea," I responded, recalling my dear coffee mug. "What about an armadillo perched atop the giant blood-shot eyeball? Its tough shell symbolizes the character armor we must bear against corporate crime." Naturally, I was still opposed to society's mediocrity (the original enemy of my armadillo mug). But sometimes larger issues come to the fore.

We finished our new logo design and fine-tuned the up-dates. We had another hour before the late edition of the paper came out, so we relaxed a bit. Jeff insisted on taking a shower in his spotlight bathroom. He said he had not showered in days and wanted to be fresh and squeaky tomorrow when the Place read the newspaper article. I sat at the computer and wrote a letter of complaint to my landlord.

Dear Mr. Lionakis,

Although you have provided us with running water most months and permission to beautify your yard, which in turn will raise your property value and accordingly our rent, I must protest against our surly and incompetent janitoress. Presumably, you did not hire Jadwiga to sit on the front stoop, smoke, and make smart comments to the tenants, yet that is the unfortunate situation at present. The hallways are a disgrace, and cobwebs are all too visible between the sixth and seventh banister posts on the third floor. In addition, a slice of cotto salami laid on the carpet in front of the washing machine for four days until one of the rats finally carted it away. I abhor tattle-tales, but we all know Jadwiga's fondness for piquant lunch-meats.

Mr. Lionakis, there are many illegal immigrants in our neighborhood; won't you give one of them the chance to clean our building properly?

Regards,
Mr. Chung

I think I used just the right combination of authority and politeness. I don't want to infuriate the man, as he is part of a powerful cabal of Greek landlords who wield might through-out Chicago like a burning platter of saganaki.

I had printed out the letter and slipped it into my thread-bare knockoff Kate Spade handbag when I heard a sound at Jeff's door. As I turned, I saw, through the transparent shower curtains surrounding the tub, Jeff's fleshy bulk scrubbing away. Ugh, my stomach lurched in response. Beyond, I could just see the hovel door creaking open, inch by inch. A skinny leg in white jeans stepped through silently, followed by a mangy paw. Frightened, I hid under the computer desk. Damn

Fat Bald Jeff and his sudden need for cleanliness! Over the running water, he couldn't hear the landlady's son advance. I scrunched farther underneath the desk, watching the dog sniff around unleashed. The guy poked around in Jeff's milk crates for a minute, then spied his nemesis hosing off in the middle of the room.

"Heh, heh," the creep chuckled softly. "Come, Kong." Kong first ran into one of the load-bearing pillars in the loft, then trotted up to his master. My eyes were glued to Jeff, willing him to snap out of it. He continued to scrub. How many layers of grime could there be?

"Gonna git it now, fat boy," said the ruffian, and he whispered to the mongrel, holding it by its scruff. The twosome crept forward and the dog began to growl.

In the bathroom, Jeff reached for a towel. Chaos erupted!

The landlady's son tore open the shower curtain and released his hold on Kong, who leapt up with frothy verve. At the same moment, Fat Bald Jeff bounced out of the metal tub, brandishing a samurai sword high above his head, completely nude and extremely moist.

Dog came up. Sword came down. I shrieked and hid behind my hands. Moments later, as I peeked fearfully through my fingers, I saw the trailer-trash philistine run screaming from the hovel, arms flailing above his head, as Fat Bald Jeff stood above a mass of gore. Blood poured out of a stump where the mongrel's head had once been!

Chapter 9

Head throbbed. Felt feverish. Fat Bald Jeff doesn't own any sort of wheeled vehicle, so he made me sit in my plastic handlebar basket as he pedaled us hell for leather to my house. The neighborhood toughs watched us as we sped down the street at ninety miles an hour: an enormously fat man riding a pink girl's bike, Austin Powers shoved in the front basket. I hit my head on a low-hanging tree branch and probably would have been knocked out but for the motorcycle helmet.

The busybodies in 2F stuck their heads out of their doorway and peeped down at Jeff and me as we wrestled for the bike in the lobby.

"Just leave it here!" he exploded.

"I can't! Everything must go in its proper place," I cried. First it's bikes in the lobby, then it's crack dealers in the hallway; from there, a short step to feral cats overrunning the building.

Jeff wrested the bike out of my feeble grasp and threw it down the basement stairs. It made a horrible racket as it clattered and bounced off the steps and landed in a mangled heap at the entrance to the laundry room.

The misfortune with the tree branch had made me woozy, and I crumpled to the floor in agony.

"Come on," urged Jeff, "get up." I said I couldn't and for him to go on without me, but I expect my voice was muffled from the helmet because he ignored my pleas and hoisted me fireman-style over his shoulder to carry me up the stairs.

Upside down, I saw 2F and hideous Alma enjoying the show. Jeff made a quick turn and I banged my head on the handrail. Only the motorcycle helmet saved me from permanent injury.

Mr. Chung asked, "What happened? Is that blood on her?"

Jeff said, "I couldn't begin to explain."

"Rough sex," Alma summed up succinctly and shut her door, dragging all her furniture across the room to block the door.

"Do you need help?" asked Stefan.

"I think so," huffed Jeff, "she weighs a lot more than she looks."

"It's all in the helmet," replied Chung, and the three of them had a nice chuckle as I dangled from Jeff's shoulder, screaming into a black hole of social oblivion.

Together they got me up the last flight and dumped me in front of my door. I rolled around on the floor, trying to right myself, as 2F wrote out an invitation to Jeff for their big party next month.

"Bring a date," they said, "but not . . . you know." I believe some gesture was made, then I heard 2F giggle their way down the stairs. I struggled and got my head stuck between the banister posts.

Upon hearing the ruckus, Val Wayne opened the door. Jeff cleared his throat.

"Hi, remember me? Fat Bald Jeff, and uh, I think Addie needs some help . . ." Jeff's voice trailed off as he tried to explain why I was covered in gore. Val, I must say, handled the situation with admirable efficiency. After releasing me from the banister posts, he ordered me into the shower to clean off the blood. He prepared mugs of hot milk and whiskey for us and set out extra blankets and pillows on the disco couch. Once settled, he asked Jeff for the full account. He silenced me several times as I tried to add my two cents; he declared my version incoherent though imaginative.

"All I know is, I heard a noise—Addie's incessant chatter had stopped some minutes before—and I instinctively reached for the samurai sword," said Jeff. He trembled a bit and pulled the afghan closer around him.

"Purely defensive," said Val, nodding. "Go on."

"Well, when the shower curtain opened, I jumped out, saw the dog, and held the sword out in front of me. They always say you should put something between you and an attacking dog."

"A sharp blade is a good thing," encouraged Val.

"He was completely nude," I whispered.

"I was in the shower!"

Val told me to shut up and drink my whiskey. I obeyed, but I knew that that vision would never leave me.

"All right, so you had the sword out. The . . . inevitable resulted, right? Your neighbor ran out screaming. Then what?"

Fat Bald Jeff swallowed with difficulty. "We had to clean up the mess. It could have dripped down into the landlady's apartment, and she'd stick me with the cleaning bill.",

"I haven't had my dinner," I said. They looked at me as if I were mad.

"My digestion—" I began, but they both held up their hands to stop me. Val shook me.

"Do you have any concept of what's going on here?" he yelled right in my face. He had new follicles sprouting in his bare patch.

"I'm sorry," I whimpered, "but I get very nervous when I haven't eaten. I feel faint and dizzy. May I lie down here? Jeff, could you just move over an eensy bit? Thank you."

Val stomped into the kitchen and returned with half a kielbasa. He shoved it in my hand and warned me not to say another word. I was grateful for the sausage. It was a bit fatty for my tastes, but I dared not say a thing!

Jeff continued, "We wrapped up the head and the body in two bedsheets, and I put them in front of the landlady's son's door. I didn't know what else to do with them. Maybe he would want to bury them. Nobody was around. Addie mopped up the blood." He looked at me appreciatively.

"She *is* good at cleaning," Val Wayne grudgingly replied.

Well, I ruined my pedal pushers and pink gingham blouse. They would have to go in the trash. Why couldn't I have been wearing the sari during the bloodbath? But I never could have ridden my bicycle in the sari. Thoughts crowded into my head and I groaned. Jeff hadn't ruined any of his stupid black clothes, as he went outside in his birthday suit to deliver the carcass. I suppose I should be glad he bothered to put on any clothes at all for our bike ride home.

Val refilled our mugs and asked what I was doing at Jeff's so late on a weeknight.

Immediately I blurted out the truth, Crook-Eye website and all.

"You stupid idiot!" screamed Jeff. "I told you to keep your trap shut."

I wailed, "I'm sorry, I can't hold up under heavy interrogation."

He sputtered, "*That* was heavy interrogation?"

I buried my head under the blanket and sobbed miserably. "You don't know Val."

But Val, of course, thought the website was hilarious and, in any event, would not blab. He firmly told Jeff to sleep at our apartment tonight; there was no telling what would be waiting for him back at his hovel.

In the middle of the night, I awoke to a desperate cry coming from the living room. I sprang from bed and ran out there. Jeff was thrashing about on the couch, moaning in his sleep.

Tried to shake him out of his dream, but to no effect. Yelling his name produced no result either, so I grabbed one of our fondue forks from the kitchen fondue nook and jabbed him repeatedly in the chest.

He woke up.

"Stop poking me," he said irritably, sitting up. I switched on the light and gasped. Again, he was completely naked! I don't understand the modern fascination with nudity; I am never nude.

Averting my eyes, I draped the afghan over Jeff's tumescence and explained that he was having a bad dream. I omitted that it was a very loud dream and had deprived me of much-needed rest, as he had had a tough night.

"Ugh," he groaned, "I dreamt that the mongrel had come back from the front stoop to haunt me. It was carrying its own head in your bicycle basket."

We were both quiet for a moment as Jeff arranged himself under the blanket and gulped the last sip of his partially curdled milk and whiskey. Then we heard it. A low, mournful yowl coming from outside. Jeff's eyebrows shot up into his oily globe. I explained about the white puppy next door.

He said, "So you haven't done anything about it? You just listen to it night after night?"

I replied that the animal officials were supposedly handling it, since I, unlike some people, cannot solve domestic animal problems with a samurai sword.

His eyes strayed to the fondue fork in my hand. His stomach gurgled obtrusively.

"Mmmm," he said, "fondue."

After what Fat Bald Jeff had done for me in terms of workplace liberation and increased self-esteem, I felt it was not asking too much to make him a bubbling kettle of fondue.

"Stale millet bread okay with you?" I asked, cutting it up into little cubes.

Had a nice snack together, despite the fact that three-thirty A.M. is not one of my prescribed meal times. But since my day's eating schedule had been wrecked by the late night kielbasa, I figured, why not? I am becoming more daring and devil-may-care with the passage of each day.

Fat Bald Jeff and I rode the bus together to work. In the front there was a single empty seat, in which he promptly stuffed himself. I sent a lukewarm poison dart his way but recalled it, considering what he'd been through the previous night.

He looked up at me, half-rose, and said, "Oh. Please take it."

"No, no," I replied politely, preparing to sit anyway.

He shrugged, plopped back down, and took out a paperback titled *101 Things to Do Till the Revolution*. Doesn't he understand the elaborate etiquette dance our society has devised?

When we reached the Place, we could hardly get through the crowd. Two TV news crews had staked themselves outside the building, and sleepy, unarmed Earl stood sentry at the doors, checking staff IDs. We passed through and entered the lobby. Zombies were swarming in a near panic.

"What's going on?" I asked Jeff above the din.

He gave me a crafty smile and said, "The biscotti are burning."

"I don't understand this metaphor anymore," I complained. "Are the biscotti *people* or the *plan*, because—"

His smile distorted into a tense grimace, and he spoke through clamped jaws. "Shut up. Figure it out yourself. I'll find you later." And he disappeared into the crowd. I waited for the elevator to take me to the second floor. The doors slid open. The interior of the elevator was covered in BONGS NOT BOMBS stickers.

On the second floor, publishing was in turmoil! Someone had roped off the entrance to Coddles's office, restricting the zombies crowding in the hallway. Throughout the department I heard mingled laughter, screaming, and crying. Pushed my way down the corridor to my cubicle. The noise was so deafening I couldn't even hear the constant, annoying hum of the fluorescent lights. Logged on and saw my e-mail in box flooded with messages intended for all staff. The executive director condemned Crook-Eye, Ltd., and its libelous blasphemies (ha!), particularly the article about how she violated the public relations high school intern last year in the executive coat closet. Interns, ignored by practically everyone, often make friends with the mailroom staff and disclose vital information.

Bev and Lura came into my cubicle to relay the latest news.

"The board has put the executive director under investigation!" cried Bev.

Lura added, "And most of the department heads and some of the unit heads, including Coddles."

"Where is Coddles?" I asked. "Barricaded in his office?"

They shrugged. Imagine barricading yourself in a room filled with Italian Provincial furniture!

The halls were filled with meandering zombies. Nobody was working. It was all because of Fat Bald Jeff and me!

Down in the graphic designer wing, I noticed this morning's *Sun-Times* on the conference table. Front-page scandal, complete with Coddles's disgusting hobbies! Picked it up and hurried over to Francis's cubicle, when I noticed that all the nameplates on the walls had been covered with political slogan stickers. Many of them had MUMIA crossed out and replaced with BIG LOU.

"Did you see the newspaper?" I asked, sitting down in the folding chair opposite Francis.

For a few minutes we happily discussed the turmoil. Francis said a lunchtime candlelight vigil had been planned in the dungeon around Big Lou's old locker. Perhaps this was the next step in Big Lou's vindication and eventual reinstatement. He was a nice fellow and had often invited the lower-rung publishing staff to clandestine poker games held by junior maintenance crew in the boiler room after hours. They played for M&M's, and if gassy Bev hadn't always joined in, I might have participated.

"Everyone seems to have copied your Mumia and bong stickers," I said, picking invisible lint off the frilly placket of my count of Monte Cristo blouse.

"Well," he replied, absently searching for Cheerios in his hair, "actually, I put them up myself."

I looked at him uneasily, sensing the approaching inquest.

He leaned in earnestly and whispered, "It's okay. I know. You're Crook-Eye, aren't you?"

But before I could deny or admit anything under his brutal inquisition, Bev burst into Francis's cubicle.

"Did you hear?" she shrieked. "Coddles is dead! He threw himself in front of an El train."

Absolutely frantic, I tore down the back stairwell. *That's* how disturbed I was—did not even *think* of using the elevator! I needed a few moments' rest once I reached the dungeon, but there was nothing to sit on but a dusty old computer box, and I'd forgotten my hanky.

Fat Bald Jeff was sitting calmly at his workstation, typing away as though nothing was out of the ordinary. I attempted to run past the administrative desk geek guarding the Hole, but he barred my ingress.

"You cannot just waltz—"

I interrupted, breathless. "I know, sorry. I just wanted to ask Jeff a question."

The frail geek sucked his gums and teeth dry as he glared at me, two spots of puce blotching his gray cheeks.

"Fat Bald, Fat Bald," I added quickly.

He groaned into the intercom microphone. "Fat Bald Jeff, please come to the administration desk. Fat Bald Jeff, to the administration desk."

The geek stiffly settled back in his chair and regarded me coldly. Jeff took his sweet old time getting to the glass door.

I smiled at the desk nerd; perhaps he just needed a little kindness to bring him out of his horrible geek shell. "I just noticed we have the same spectacles," I began, resting my elbows on the desk.

He gave a dry little cough. "They're dismantling our department. Please do not rest your limbs on my desk."

Fat Bald Jeff finally came and rescued me. Other Jeff hovered anxiously around us as we walked back over to the workstations. His RON'S PIZZA baseball cap had finally come apart in the back and was held together with packing tape.

Other Jeff said, "What am I going to do? No one else will ever hire me."

Fat Bald Jeff said kindly, "They can't fire all of us. And nobody here will work for *your* wages." Placated, Other Jeff went back to his cubicle. Fat Bald Jeff and I went over to his desk, where he began working at his computer. I chewed my thumbnails.

"They're dismantling your department?" I asked.

"Yeah, no biggie."

Then I burst out with the awful news. "Jeff, Coddles is dead."

"Yes, I heard," he said mildly. He continued to type, his fat fingers darting about the keyboard like overstuffed crappie trawling for chum.

"He threw himself in front of the El!" I said. "And it's all our—"

He stopped typing and silenced me with a look that would freeze the sun. My stomach rumbled nervously. It was 12:06.

He cleared his throat and resumed typing. "He accidentally fell in its path this morning on the way to work. He was reading the *Sun-Times* as he walked down the platform, engrossed in some article, and tumbled right onto the track as the Evanston Express roared by."

Evanston! How cruel and ironic fate is.

"He didn't kill himself?"

"Not that I'm aware of," said Jeff. "Didn't you see the e-mail Miss Fernquist posted at eleven-thirty?" He brought it up onscreen for me to read.

To: All staff

From: L. Fernquist, publishing

As you may have heard, our colleague—and my dear boss—Albert Barr passed away this morning. Some of you called him Coddles. Contrary to what some employees have been saying, Albert *accidentally* stepped in front of the El. It's a shame that he left our world without being able to clear his good name of the lies printed about him on the Internet. I don't know who these Crook-Eye jerks are, but they don't speak for me. Albert was a real good boss, and to you bitches in the secretarial pool: I got promoted over you because I'm good with shorthand and for no other reason.

Also, Albert was a big fan of the El, as you can see by

the following e-mail I just received, and if he was going to kill himself, he wouldn't use the train.

To: Miss Fernquist, secretary to Albert Barr
From: Ian el-Sabbah, CTA Red Line manager
I wish to convey my deep sadness about the Evanston Express tragedy this morning. I can't tell you the number of times passengers have stumbled onto the rails while reading the *Sun-Times*. I manage the Red Line, not the Express, and of course I am in no way liable for this accident and in fact boast a reasonably good record regarding chance casualties on my line. I had a special ongoing dialogue with Mr. Barr about the standard of excellence on the El, and I appreciated his frequent, lengthy criticisms about my ability to do my job. I am pleased that your boss had not given up on us at the Chicago Transit Authority, even though his complaints were unwavering and rambling and somewhat psychotic. Of course, if he had only stayed away from the El as he threatened to do numerous times, this whole unfortunate business would have been avoided. But I will always recall with fondness our correspondence, and hope you will pass along my condolences to his grandmother, to whom he was exceedingly attached.

> Sincerely,
> Ian el-Sabbah, soon to be promoted
> to Evanston Express manager

"I don't feel so good," I whimpered, clutching my stomach. Fat Bald Jeff checked his watch.

"Oh, yes. It's a quarter past twelve. I'm going to pick up some beer brats for Big Lou's candlelight vigil, if you'd like one. Coming?"

I shook my head. I wanted to talk more about Coddles, but Jeff warned me to keep my mouth shut and we'd discuss it later in private. Lurched blindly to the elevator. Coddles—dead! I couldn't help but feel responsible.

Of course he was repugnant. And it wasn't just the kiddie porn and yucko diapers, it was his slave-driving tactics, his disregard for the well-being of his employees. I shouldn't worry about Coddles, right? I should worry about Fat Bald Jeff, working for a pittance, living in a grotty attic, fending off the advances of mad landladies and mongrels. Yet I did feel guilty about my supervisor. It's almost as though I pushed him off the platform myself, though heaven knows that in reality my upper body strength is geriatric at best. Maybe there was a Mrs. Coddles weeping over the loss of her breadwinner. I wanted to be a rabble-rouser, not a Coddles-killer. If I hadn't started Crook-Eye with Jeff, Coddles would probably be here right now, eyeing my bosom and working me into my grave. Now he's roasting in hell. It's my fault. It's not my fault. Is it my fault?

This cannot be good for my digestion.

Brought my egg salad on millet bread into my cube and ate lunch. The events of the past twenty-four hours made my head swim, and I couldn't face eating in the editorial lounge. Plus the temp had fallen asleep at his desk in the common area, and truth be told, poor fellow, he really did stink.

By one o'clock I'd had enough. None of the journals I edited had come back from layout, and I had nothing to do and nobody to boss me. Went home (lousy bus is not so bad in the middle of the day), changed into grubby pumpkin-farmer pants, plain polo-necked shirt, and childish white gym sneakers, and went into the garden to work. Paco was out there, making manure tea.

He asked if I was playing "hooker" from work today. Instead of correcting his English, which would have been the kinder, more constructive thing, I just nodded. I cannot take responsibility for assimilating immigrants into our culture, any more than I can take responsibility for what newspapers people choose to read while standing so close to the El tracks. It wasn't my fault. It was totally my fault. Oh, hell.

Decided not to put my poisonous plants so close to Alma's stinko mustard greens. True, she is awful and probably longs for the solace of the cemetery, but I could not face going to jail on murder charges. All that denim and subordination, not to mention the lecherous cell-block matrons and thin gruel. I would not last a day in prison! I couldn't fashion a knife out of a toothbrush if my life depended upon it.

Alma shrieked instructions at me from her back porch. She wanted her rows of watercress perfectly straight and verbally abused me until I had planted them right. Meanwhile, Paco kept shouting, "Playing hooker!" and pointing at me.

Alma shouted back, "Don't have to tell *me*!"

Our society is in shambles due to the incivility of our elderly citizens.

Took out Alma's garbage. She tossed it at me as I came up the stairs, so I had no choice. A clear plastic bag stuffed with horrible clothes from her extra room sat outside her door, so I asked her if she wanted me to throw those out as well.

"That's my laundry, girl!" Alma barked.

Someone should tell Alma that all her shouting will only give her a coronary, but you can bet that it won't be me. Before she could ask me to wash her disgusting garments, I ran up the stairs. Did not warn her about lazy Jadwiga nor the pastrami hanging from the drying rack. Just my luck that 2F opened their door as I passed. Does no one work in this building?

They stared at me curiously. I stared back. I had mud smudged across my nose and my manicure was a wreck, but frankly I no longer cared. Life was taking a strange turn for me, and I could not be bothered with mundane concerns.

Chung held the *Sun-Times* in his hand. "Don't you work at this place?" he asked, pointing to the article on the front page. I said I did and prayed for the battery of questions to stop there.

Stefan stepped into the hallway and eyeballed me. He asked if I was all right.

"Of course I am. Why shouldn't I be? I had nothing to do with that website! Nothing! He fell in front of a train. I don't know anything."

He blinked a few times then said, "I meant about your accident last night. You were covered in blood and that big guy carried you up the stairs, remember?"

"Oh, that. Yes, I'm fine. Who would have known the old dog had so much blood in him?" I wisecracked lamely. They exchanged glances. Nobody understands my Shakespearean jokes.

They continued to stare as I walked up the last flight. I could feel the fire from their eyes on my back as I turned the corner, and a moist, salty substance drenched my forehead.

The scrutiny weighed heavily upon me, and my hand shook as I fumbled with my keys. Francis's face floated before me ... I mumbled to myself like a madman, confessing to the murder of King Duncan, not to mention all those Scottish women and children. A tiny click sounded and my will broke under the strain.

"Yes, I admit it! It was me all along!" I screamed. But they had already closed their door, and my confession rang hollowly in the empty stairway.

When Val Wayne came home, he found the apartment shining and clean. I, too, was shining and clean after a nice hot shower, facial mud pack, hot oil hair treatment, pedicure, elbow loofah, and a change into freshly hand-laundered pink silk pajamas. I suppose I still *do* care a tiny bit about mundane concerns. After all, a good scrubbing settles a tense mind.

"What's going on?" he called from his bedroom, changing into his household uniform. "I saw the newspaper at lunch."

I explained all the recent developments. Val listened carefully while grooming his sprouting mustache. It's filled in a bit. He looks more like Apollo Creed now instead of John Waters.

"Addie, I'm so proud of you," he said. "I mean, I'm sorry your boss got run over, but that wasn't really your fault. That website—I looked it over today at the office, and I have to say it's brilliant. I never knew you could write. And think what good you've done for the other peons at work, especially the janitor."

Yes. One must think of the janitors (except Jadwiga), and not of oneself and how terrified one might be of getting caught and going to jail. But Val said nobody would ever in a million years suspect me or Fat Bald Jeff. We weren't outwardly thought of as rabble-rousers, nor were we considered the least bit clever by our superiors.

"You're a freedom fighter." Val smiled. "Like Mumia Abu-Jamal." I flushed with pride. See where having a bad attitude and hating work can lead you?

We were interrupted by the sound of our buzzer. Val went to the intercom, then informed me the Lemming was on his way up. He threw Deep Purple on the stereo full volume and settled into the disco couch with half a lime shoved in his mouth.

"We might want a little privacy," I said.

He gestured expansively toward my bedroom. *That* sort of privacy only encourages the Lemming to disrobe and convulse around me. I just wanted some quiet for conversation.

I opened our door and he stepped in. As usual, he wore his conservative suit and stained rep tie. It occurred to me that I have never seen the Lemming in anything but a suit, not counting the times when his pants were draped around his ankles in the backseat of his car. Does he even own casual sportswear? Suddenly, an image flashed before me of the Lemming parading about in Francis's acrylic grandpa sweater, and I stifled a laugh.

The Lemming gave me a dry peck on the cheek, acne scars and huge pores looming, and the laughter disintegrated in my throat.

"Hello, darling. Hello, Val Wayne Newton," he greeted.

Val removed the lime from his mouth and threw it at the Lemming. It hit him as sure as if there were a target drawn on his forehead. The Lemming has the dull physical reflexes of an investment banker.

"You know I don't like that," said Val angrily. "Val. Val Wayne. Even Val Newton. But not Val Wayne Newton!"

The Lemming dabbed at his forehead with a handkerchief, feigning ignorance. "Settle down. I had no idea."

"It's a family name," replied Val. "I just can't stand my family."

Quickly I fixed us all some Bloody Marys. There is no fire that can't be quenched with a little alcohol. I led the Lemming into my bedroom and closed the door. The frontal expansion on his trousers was immediate and disgusting.

"Ick," he said, placing the drink on my nightstand. "Tastes like inferior rib-eye steak." He flung himself on my bed and sighed. He held his arms out in feeble command, and I reluctantly laid down in them. I couldn't get comfortable. The Lemming is all bones and teeth and coarse fibers.

He said, "I heard about all the trouble at your office."

I said nothing.

"What a stupid prank. I mean, who cares?" He yawned. "You probably did it, didn't you."

"Of course not," I answered, banishing thoughts of Duncan and Banquo and all those dead Thanes.

He stuck his pointy nose deep into my neck in a strangling attempt at cuddling. "I wasn't serious."

No, he wouldn't be. Val and Jeff have no problem believing there could be something deep and riotous and thrilling inside me. But the Lemming sees me only as a shallow brat with a fine clavicle.

Then he looked around, assessing my room full of junk. "You have *got* to throw out this hideous pom-pom bedspread and that perfectly ridiculous lamp your father made that doesn't even work, not to mention your three-legged dresser."

"The lamp works. You just have to jiggle the cord."

"Darling," he said, "it's the worst example of Arts and Crafts I've ever seen."

It was one thing when *I* mocked Father's lousy pottery. For years I had to pick clay out of my hair and food while the kiln belched out Maoist chess pieces. Yes, he was foolish and weird, but as Gran said, he always loved his little princess. Me. I was a princess, at least in my father's bleary eyes. The Lemming is merely a priss, and when he makes fun of my father, it just sounds mean.

I said tentatively, "Well, I like the lamp. But I would also like that Sheraton mahogany passed down from prior Lemmings."

"I know you covet my furniture. I don't blame you. It's what you've always wanted." He breathed humidly into my ear, struggling out of his pants.

I sighed. "I've always wanted a sprawling Tudor castle, preferably moated and ancestral."

He grunted in assent, or maybe it was a grunt of frustration at not being able to disengage his pants from his feet. He kicked and kicked to no avail. I sat up to untie his wingtips.

"But what good is a nice house and nice stuff when there's just a lot of boring people hanging around all the time?" I mused, dropping the shoes to the ground.

"Uh-huh," he said, pitching his suit coat in the corner, following it with his tie.

I unbuttoned his dress shirt absently. "Even this build-ing doesn't seem so bad when Val's around, or when we're all working in the yard together."

"That's the place," he said, moving my hands to his de-pressing pelvic area.

"Right, even the *Place* is tolerable now that I know Fat Bald Jeff and Francis," I agreed. The Lemming occasionally makes good sense. "Of course," I continued, "who knows what will happen there now?"

"So what do you think about all this?" he asked.

"Tomorrow at work I'll probably have a better idea—"

"No, no," he admonished me sharply. *"This."*

Oh. *That.*

Concave and hairless, and all yucky beluga-pale.

He clasped me to his chest, shoving a bunch of knuckles all over me. "Take your clothes off," he begged.

"They're not clothes, they're pajamas," I said. And I didn't spend $39.99 at the Lord & Taylor intimate-apparel clearance sale so I could end up tossing them on the floor.

The Lemming brought my face down to his and gasped, "Oh mama."

Suddenly my bedroom door burst open. The Lemming shrieked a womanly scream and tried to cover himself with my hideous pom-pom bedspread. Fat Bald Jeff stood in my doorway with a profound look of embarrassment.

"Oh! Sorry," gulped Jeff, his moon face turning alternate shades of scarlet and purple. "Val said you weren't doing anything in here."

"They usually aren't," called Val from the kitchen. "Addie's frigid."

How dare he! "I'm *particular*," I interjected.

The Lemming retorted, "What's that supposed to mean?"

Jeff said, "I think I'll go."

"No, wait," I said, climbing off the Lemming, who immediately burrowed under the bedspread. "Is everything all right?" I motioned for Jeff to sit next to me on the bed. Val followed him in with the tray of drinks.

"Bloodies, anyone?" offered Val.

"Get out! Everyone get out!" shrieked the Lemming from under the covers.

"Just a sec," I said, distributing the beverages.

Fat Bald Jeff said that after the candlelight vigil at Big Lou's locker, in which a minor mishap involving the Hibachi, lit candles, and a carelessly placed bottle of 151 set off the fire alarms and sent all staff fleeing for the exits (fully documented by the news crews), a "crisis memo" had alerted certain departments of imminent layoffs.

"Did you lose your job?" I asked fearfully.

"No," he said, staring into his glass, "but you did."

I cried for a while as Jeff and Val comforted me. The Lemming continued to kick and thrash under the bedspread, but in my state I could scarcely be bothered.

Finally he sat up and asked hoarsely, "Do you mind moving your encounter session out to the living room so I can get my pants on?"

Val Wayne volunteered to cook up a pot of spaghetti and sautéed vegetables. Would have done it myself, but it was nearly forty minutes past my usual dinnertime and I felt too weak and bewildered to stand over a hot stove and stir things.

"Don't bother making any for me," said Jeff. "I have to go home now."

I looked at him in shock. "To the hovel? You can't! What if that fiend is waiting there to avenge his mongrel's death?"

Jeff considered. He said, "I can't help that. The hovel is my home." This was said with characteristic humility. I so admired that Fat Bald Jeff. He was truly brave.

The Lemming stormed out of my bedroom, disheveled and ornery. He fixed his tie with ineffective little jerks in the mirror by the door.

"I lost my job," I sniveled. "I'm destitute."

He said to me, "That's the way the ball bounces. I'd lend you money, but I never carry cash. Anyway, Addie, I'll be traveling on business for a couple weeks, but I'll be back for that party."

"For what?" I asked.

He gave a yank of impatience to his tie and nearly asphyxiated himself. He bit the words off as though speaking to an idiot child. "For the goddamn party the fags are giving."

And with that, he stomped out and slammed the door.

I turned to Val and whimpered in disbelief, "2F invited *him* and not *me*?"

Val shrugged and turned back to the saucepan, but I saw the smug grin on his face!

"Hey," he said, "that's the way the bong bounces." And he fired up a monster joint and laughed himself sick.

Threw myself on the disco couch, preparing to tantrum, but no one was watching, and anyway, I was exhausted from all the lovemaking.

Chapter 10

Those of us laid off still had to come in for another week to clean out our cubicles, finish what work we could, and delegate all unfinished tasks. Mr. Genett had organized a memorial service in the conference room to commemorate our late unit head, then explained the layoffs.

"Sorry," he said, not sounding a *bit* sorry, "but after all the brouhaha with that website and the resultant bad press and, uh, legal ramifications, all departments have to pare down. What with the costs incurred by imprudent use of the company credit card and so on and so forth, publishing will be keeping only one employee in each of its units. " At least Bev was booted out along with me; I was glad Lura and Francis got to keep their jobs. Mr. Genett decided to keep most of the production slaves so they could take up the slack left by departing coworkers. The production slaves looked rather proud of themselves for once. They didn't yet realize that they would not be compensated for all the extra work! The cycle was starting over again, although they would never object. Zombies, by definition, never question poor work conditions.

Tech support kept the Jeffs, as they had seniority and didn't protest pay cuts.

I stayed under the afghan on the disco couch for ages.

Val was very sympathetic and told me he would handle the rent until I got another job. Wasn't sure what kind of job

I would be good at. The only thing I'd found that I liked to do was write mean things about people on the website.

Weeks passed in this fashion: resting on the disco couch—gathering strength for the next sickening job, whatever it would be—bravely venturing out to Arturo's Seafood and Liquor Shop for sustenance, eating take-out pizza (wheat crust, soysage) with Lura, Francis, and Jeff every Wednesday evening, taking the El downtown to Marshall Field's for the thirteen-hour sale (maxed out MasterCard—stupid thousand-dollar limit—found gorgeous irregular Donna Karan camp shirt, very good for future work wardrobe, left sleeve can be shortened), sipping iced tea in the backyard while ignoring Alma's screeching re: weedy veg patch, and getting Val to drive me to Gran's (too weak for the Red Line).

But all that began to change the day Val came home from work and handed me the envelope. It was addressed to the two of us, and he sat next to me on the couch while I opened it. Removed an engraved invitation, read it silently, passed it to Val, then retreated under the afghan.

He read aloud the awful news.

THE PLEASURE OF YOUR COMPANY
IS REQUESTED AT THE MARRIAGE OF
RUTH ANDERSON PREWITT
TO
JANN MATTHIAS HELLSTROM

"This is upsetting to you?" he asked.

"I don't know," I murmured. "Kind of."

He pulled the afghan off my head. "Why? Didn't she tell you?"

"Well, I think she sort of mentioned it a few times, but I may have blocked it out—"

"You better stop feeling sorry for yourself," ordered Val. "And stop lying around here all day."

"Why?" I asked listlessly. My arm flopped off the couch, but I just left it on the floor amidst the dust bunnies.

"Because it's not healthy," said Val.

I sighed in response. What would Val know about health, anyway? He is a stranger to regular mealtimes and nutritious eating.

"You don't know how good you have it," he said. "So your mom's getting married. So what?"

"She's marrying the hulking Nordo. I have no career. Nobody loves me."

"You dumb-ass. You really are a *dumb-ass*. You have me here helping you instead of kicking your lazy flat butt out. Francis and Lura and Fat Bald Jeff come by all the time to visit. And speaking of Fat Bald Jeff, have you even stopped to think how grateful you should be to him for the Crook-Eye project? Sometimes, Addie, I feel like smacking you right in the mouth." I hoped he would not smack me in the mouth. My bucks give me a sad-bunny look that subdues most aggression, but Val can be very unpredictable.

"You found something you were good at, you took a stand against the bullshit that happens to peons at work, and you're not even happy. The only thing you've lost is a crappy job you hated anyway. You have friends, the world's most tolerant roommate, a cool mother. She calls every day to check on you. When's the last time *my* mother called here?"

Felt ashamed. Val's parents moved to Portland last year and forgot all about him.

He slumped on the couch next to me. "They've never even invited me out there."

We don't talk about the Newtons. Now that Val and his siblings are all in their twenties, their parents kind of dumped them and just took off. On holidays he comes with me to Gran's or goes to his brother's condo in the suburbs or sometimes stays home by himself, hoping his mom and dad will call. They don't know he has a new paralegal job, or that he passed out dehydrated at my birthday party last year and needed twelve stitches in his chin. My mother and Jann drove him to the hospital.

"You're not missing anything in convention-flouting Oregon," I said, resting my head against him.

"I know," he said.

"I hated living there," I continued.

"Look, I know, Addie. Can you just sit here a while and shut up?"

At the end of my family's on-the-road living experiment, we ended up at the long-sought commune in Eugene, Oregon. Endless months of communal peanut butter, performing natural functions out in the open, and minimal bathing concluded at a bonfire celebrating the autumnal equinox. The parents were dancing around the fire with the other idle layabouts. I sat with my back toward the hippies, filing my toenails with a piece of river rock. As usual, they started bickering over who would have to leave the party and put me to bed. Mother lost the argument and dragged me by the hand to our cabin. Surely other mothers, somewhere, delighted in spending bedtime with their children. She groaned and complained the whole way through the woods that she had never been able to do anything for herself—everything she did was for her husband, her child, the commune, and Grandmother. I found that a little melodramatic; when we still lived in our old house, she was always gadding about to the grocery store and block club meetings.

"When is it time for *me*?" she whined. She had the right attitude for the eighties, except we were stuck in the inhuman conditions of nature instead of industrialized civilization, like normal people.

She pushed me into my bunk and said maybe if my father ever helped her with me, she'd be a lot easier to get along with. She stalked out of the cabin, treading on Father's homeopathic remedies strewn about the floor. I sobbed—like I had so many other times—into my indestructible hemp pillow. Ventured out of the cabin shortly thereafter, with only my pillow and Bob Marley quilt to protect me against marauding brown bears. I wanted to punish the parents for leaving me in the cabin, yet I didn't want to expose myself to woodland bugs creeping around under the evergreens. So I laid down in the grass at the perimeter of the bonfire. It wasn't long before I heard the grunting and heaving particular to indecent relations in the nearby underbrush. I stood up to move away and saw that the grunting came from a hippie girl called Sundance and a frustrated potter called Father.

Mother stumbled upon them right after I did, and the next day we were packed and headed for home in the VW microbus.

I said, "Well, Ruth and Harvey, I expect it's all for the best."

Father turned around from the steering wheel and screamed, "Don't talk to us that way! For the time being, we're still your parents." At which point he nearly drove us over the highway median, but I felt my point was made.

Mother sat in the backseat, staring out the window and crying for hours on end while Father drove, stone-faced and silent. When it was her turn to drive, Father sat in the backseat playing his guitar and singing Phil Ochs's "I Ain't Marchin' Anymore." I sat on the wheel well, assembling homemade sanitary napkins.

This was how things ended for us on the road. Father spent a long time making it up to Mother, who forgave him eventually. The way she put it to me years afterward was that he was not such a great husband, but he was a good man.

I picked my head up off Val Wayne's shoulder. "Can I say something now?"

He sighed. "Oh, hell. What is it?"

"I'm sorry for being such a . . . such a . . . *pill*. I *am* grateful for my adventures in sabotage with Fat Bald Jeff, and you know I would be nothing without you around. I'm just disappointed in Mother. Why couldn't she have found happiness with a nice rich egghead instead of a Swedish powerlifter?"

"Why is this so difficult for you?" asked Val, exasperated. "She's in love and wants to be married. It's not like you're going to be living with them." A sudden hopeful expression transformed his features. "Are you?"

"No! But that—that lumbering Swede! He's like a barbarian, always eating giant turkey legs and not reading good books and so on. He's so . . . unintellectual."

Val said, "He's not your dad, that's for sure."

"That's not the problem," I said.

"I think," he said gently, "it is."

"That's preposterous," I snapped weakly, then went into my bedroom and closed the door. Flung myself on the hideous pom-pom bedspread. Would I have to call Jann "Papa?" I won't. Just because Mother's marrying him doesn't mean we will be any kind of family unit. I opened the drawer of my nightstand and retrieved my drink-recipe book. Right between Simpleton's Glogg and Suffering Bastard I kept a photograph of my father and me. We're at a pony ride, and I'm in the saddle wearing jeans (ugh), a striped T-shirt, and a small cowboy hat tipped at a rakish angle. Mother didn't want me to go on the pony ride (enslaving livestock, etc.), but Father convinced her.

"Come on, Ruth," he said. "Addie wants a ride. And the ponies look well fed and happy." He patted the little animal on the neck and boosted me up.

After a few turns around the ring, the ride was over. Father asked if I liked it, and I nodded yes enthusiastically. I've always been a very simple girl at heart.

"Wait," called Mother before I dismounted. "Let's get a picture of Priss on the pony." Father and I were amazed that Mother wanted to document the livestock enslavement, but we smiled gladly for the camera. He steadied me, one hand on my arm, the other behind my head, forming rabbit ears with his fingers.

Put the photo and book back in the nightstand. Then I went to the mirror by my dresser to freshen up my face with powder and lipstick. No need for Val to see what kind of emotions had been dripping down my cheeks. Flicked on the

Arts and Crafts pottery lamp, which bathed the room in warm amber light on the first try, no cord jiggling required.

I went back in the living room. Val was packing the bowl of a three-foot bong. He said, "See what you've driven me to? I've started a new campaign to smoke a mile. Maybe by then I will be so brain-dead you won't bother me anymore." He took a huge hit. "Ah, only 5,277 feet to go."

"I think I'd like to go to the wedding," I said.

He looked at me in astonishment.

"Can we go shopping this weekend to choose a new frock?" Even though the wedding was going to be at Jann's mama's house—which stank of curing chubs and sewage from the neighboring Cal-Sag drainage ditch—I still wanted to look nice.

"Sure. Sure, of course," he said.

"Marvelous," I said, flopping down on the couch next to him. "Can you lend me some money?"

He narrowed his eyes at me but grinned in spite of himself. He was about to fire up again when I reached for the bong and said, "Could I . . . do you think I could have a little sip?"

"A sip? You mean a toke? *You?* My God! What is the world coming to?" He slapped his forehead in mock amazement, but handed it over to me.

I shrugged and lit the bowl. I've read it's good for the digestion.

Someone came knocking on our door that night. It took Val forever to get out of the shower and open it. I would have opened it myself, but I had been under a great deal of stress that day and was resting on the couch.

Mr. Chung walked in holding a sheet of paper.

"I received this from Lionakis, along with a copy of a letter I had supposedly sent him complaining about Jadwiga," he said, sitting rigidly in the Edith Bunker chair. Val sighed and went into the kitchen to make up some G&Ts.

I slid down under the afghan and asked if he could possibly come back another time, as I was convalescing and my condition could presently go either way.

"Let's hope so," he replied, handing me the landlord's letter.

Dear Mr. Chung,

Enclosing herewith your letter of last week, as leaving it on my desk at home sends my wife, Jadwiga, into hysterics. We've owned the apartment building you reside in for twenty years and regret that you find fault with our managerial style. Luckily, your lease comes up for renewal next month, at which point you may exercise the option to cancel. As for the lunch-meat issue in the laundry room, Jadwiga suggests you ask the skinny, irritable person in 3R about the sandwiches she brings downstairs while doing her wash.

Sincerely,

G. Lionakis

"George, no doubt," I said, handing back the letter. "All the Greeks are named George."

Chung stared at me, waiting, apparently, for something else. I coughed a little and smoothed down the afghan. I moved my G&T over an inch. I folded my hands across my lap. I smiled ingratiatingly. The ticking of Val's driftwood Jesus clock began to reverberate in my head. My vision clouded.

"All right!" I exploded. "It was me, I wrote it!" Covered my face with my hands but couldn't get the damn waterworks going. Dehydrated from my current ordeals, I think.

"That didn't take long," remarked Val.

"No, indeed," agreed Chung, "not long at all." They continued in this fashion as I wailed and gnashed my teeth.

Finally I stopped. I was dead tired of tantrum-ing.

"Sorry," I said, bottom lip quivering, "I just thought it would sound better coming from you. And who knew he was married to the janitoress?"

He said nothing. I felt very uncomfortable abasing myself in front of this bland, taciturn Asian. Suddenly, without meaning to, it all came spilling out: losing the job, my Crook-Eye partnership, the decapitated mongrel, dead Coddles, bossy Alma and her stinking tweeds. Anyone could see I had been suffering as of late.

Mr. Chung sat on the couch next to me. He looked at Val, gave him a curt nod, then turned to me and said, "You are an annoying little xenophobe; however, you seem to mean well, and for some reason Val Wayne likes you. You have a way with words and may possibly be clever. If you are interested, my brother—the owner of the nursery we went to—needs someone to put together his summer and fall plant catalogs. He will not pay well, but at least it's a job. I'll write out his phone number here." He did so, handed it to me, and left. Xenophobe! Leave it to the Koreans to start name-calling.

An incomprehensible look of gratitude washed over Val's face.

"Do you think this means I'm invited to their party this Friday?" I asked. Val ignored my question in favor of a more plebeian train of thought.

"What a relief." He grinned easily and dropped onto the couch with a gigantic sigh. "You could have a job. Start contributing to rent and food again. No more lying around here. No more whining like an invalid for buttered Club crackers and chicken soup. You can get out of those dirty pajamas and start treating your bedsores."

"We'll see." I sniffed. Val whipped around, tore off my afghan, and rolled me off the couch! Fell with a thump and a cry, but Val went into his bedroom and shut the door. Where was my supper of brown rice and wilted spinach? Of course, all of my recent traumas have drained my strength, physically and emotionally, and I lay on the floor for some time, trying to rally.

Got up before noon the next day, rather proud of myself. I made my own tea. Tomorrow was the big party in 2F, but I still had not received a personal invitation. Francis called me from work to tell me that he'd received his invitation via Val.

"Oh, really," I said.

"Yeah. Should I stop up at your apartment before, or—"

"No, no," I said. "I'll just see you there." Francis sounded vexed, but I did not want to be turned away at the door in front of him. 2F would probably enjoy publicly shunning me!

Fat Bald Jeff also phoned and wanted to drop by after work and bring dinner. He showed up at six o'clock with two cans of baked beans and a Bun.

He said the Place had been much subdued by our website. The worst of the bigwigs had been fired, had quit, or had died. The interim executive director, less haggish than her predecessor and possessing a streak of humanity, offered Big Lou an enviable senior maintenance position with a sizeable pay increase, but he turned it down. He had taken a job with the city as an adviser to Mayor Daley, and he liked it rather well. More temps had been hired to construct new staff nameplates—no one could remove the slogan stickers.

"I brought you this," said Jeff, reaching into his olive-drab backpack. He handed me my old signage. It still read DIE PREWITT after the sticker. He helped me put it up over the doorway to my bedroom. We stepped back to appraise our work.

"It's a little gruesome," I said.

He shrugged. "Other Jeff put up a sign that reads ARBEIT MACHT FREI over the entrance to the Hole. That's much more gruesome."

Nothing impairs my digestion more than staring at a sign that says DIE PREWITT as I eat baked beans out of a can with a spork. Jeff devoured his with gusto and hummed a little tune as he cut the Bun in half. All around, he seemed pleased with himself and the path down which he was headed.

Immediately after the beheading, the owner of the dead mongrel—terrified of Fat Bald Jeff—moved all his belongings out of the building, and Jeff hadn't seen him since. The creep was so scared of Jeff that he didn't even tell his mama (the ghastly Nibbett) what had happened to his dog. Mrs. Nibbett complained a little about the mysterious red stain she saw on Jeff's floor, but he told her it just appeared one day out of the blue, like a stigmata. I asked him if he made a deal about his rent.

He shifted in his chair and attacked the Bun. "We came to an agreement."

"What agreement?" I asked.

"Chicken Kiev once a week in her apartment, followed by cake and . . ." He trailed off and stuffed his mouth.

I finished the thought for him. "And unnatural caresses?"

He chewed his Bun ruminatively. After a full minute's silence, he curled up one side of his mouth, lifted his eyebrows, and nodded. I stared at him in horror. He couldn't mean it. Mrs. Nibbett is practically a cadaver, though less flexible.

He shrugged carelessly. "Addie, I take my opportunities as they present themselves. And the cake is really excellent."

Called Chung's Nursery about the job. The proprietor was brisk and businesslike on the phone, unlike his languorous, opulent brother. He asked me to stop by and pick up an inventory list so that I might write a few sample descriptions for his catalog. Rode my bicycle there, although the tires were wobbly after the catapult down the basement steps.

It was one of those glorious early June days. Sat outside at the picnic table with the plant list, enjoying the sunshine and light breeze. Paco grubbed around in the garden with the giantess, hoeing clods of earth. They asked for a little help, but I pointed out that I was wearing darling lilac-colored capri pants, a white cotton eyelet blouse, and lilac Prada-lookalike Mary Janes—most unsuitable for hoeing.

"Play hooker again?" asked Paco. His wife turned and gave me a look of profound disapproval.

"Er . . . yes," I replied hesitantly, as the giantess advanced.

"Good," said Paco, as I made for the door, "I like when you are around."

Worked for hours on the catalog. Discovered that it's easier to write mean things about my boss than to write informative details about ornamental kale. But I'm not complaining. I just compare the plants to people I know, and the words flow quickly. For example, the lanky rose called "White Dawn" reminds me of the Lemming, as it is pale, fussy, and not much good for bedding. Though to be fair, I wrote that it was fine up against a wall.

Called Gran to chat. She didn't know a thing about the Crook-Eye website, and although she was always supportive of me, I didn't think she would understand it or appreciate my new vocation in rebellion. Thank God she's not on the Internet and only reads the *Chicago Tribune.* All she knows is that I've got a new job writing catalog copy about plants. She thinks it's grand and that I'll be a great success in the field. Perhaps the passage of time since my dismissal has objectified my outlook, but I now think I made rather a success out of my old job as well.

"Did you receive your invitation to the wedding?" I asked.

"To eat herring with the Norwegians on the dirty South Side? Yes."

I said, "I think Mother will be happy. That's something, isn't it?"

Grandmother paused, then said, "Ruth deserves some happiness, yes. It can't have been easy with Harvey not working and making strange pots all the time. Though God knows he never showed a sign of idleness before he met your mother. Not that I pass any kind of judgment."

"Jann said we should think of him not just as a new family member, but as a skilled craftsman who will offer us design advice and architectural anecdotes for free."

"Daft boy," she said. But she sounded pleased.

Can it be that Jann possesses a sense of humor? Am now trying to reinterpret his past grunts for other meanings.

When seven-thirty on Friday struck, the Lemming rang my doorbell. He presented to me a pot specimen of French hydrangea, also known as hortensia. Pretended to fix my lipstick in the bathroom, but really went to check my *Language of Flowers* book. The secret message of hortensia? "You are cold."

For the party, Val suggested my pale blue vintage frock of shantung silk with embroidered orchids. I swept my bob behind my ears for a winning, youthful look, and tried without luck to arrange my bangs in a less International-Man-of-Mystery style. When I presented myself to the Lemming, he said I would not look good bald. What is that supposed to mean? Between his veiled insults and Val's cryptic comments, it's a wonder I have any ego left at all.

Would 2F let me in or not? A bit nervous as we knocked on 2F's door, but I reasoned that being humiliated in front of the Lemming was nothing new for me. Stefan opened the door, smiled at the Lemming, and gave me the once-over.

"Addie's my date," said the Lemming quickly.

Stefan's eyes drifted down my thrift-store outfit, taking in its full quota of dangling hem threads, too-loose bodice, and tiny stain near the neckline. I looked down at the dress, my face burning with embarrassment. What does Val know about fashion? There was a cheap smartness about my dress that told its own tale.

"Come in," he sighed.

Admittance! The party was already in full swing. There must have been at least fifty guests there already, dancing, eating, courting indiscretion. This was what I had been dreaming of, longing for, lusting over all these months. How many times I had heard their parties throbbing below, alone in my apartment, abandoned by Val, who was always an invited guest.

Gyrating in the living room to a thrilling bossa nova beat was Fat Bald Jeff. He wore a black T-shirt and jeans, as usual. Sweat flew from his glistening head in greasy beads. He punctuated the bass line by thrusting his fists into the air, biting his lower lip, and stomping both boots at once on the floor. For a massive fellow, he was surprisingly light on his feet. His dancing partner twisted mightily beside him—it was Alma, whose wretched tweed skirt flared out obscenely.

Mr. Chung had set up a makeshift bar in the kitchen, where a constantly whirring blender and five hundred liquor bottles sat on top of a giant butcher's block. The Lemming stumbled forth, arms outstretched like a sleepwalker, toward the bar. I made myself busy inspecting my neighbors' things.

Limoges china, old Wedgwood vases, Venetian goblets, and chunky Baccarat reposed in the hutch. A magnificent Hepplewhite chest stood in the bedroom. A large Sheraton settee covered in seafoam damask held three exceedingly handsome gentlemen in the far corner of the living room. I wept softly for a few minutes.

Leslie Stella

Val, adorned in his purple velvet frock coat, flared beige slacks, and Beatle boots, exuding animal magnetism, joined Fat Bald Jeff and Alma on the dance floor. The women naturally gravitated toward him. His mustache, with the help of the sable eyeliner, again looked full and lustrous and tempting. It was almost as lush as Yanni's, lucky Val!

I sat on a divine chaise in the lounge, waiting for the Lemming to bring me my drink. Mr. Chung was telling amusing stories about his trip many years ago to Andalusia, where he enjoyed some homemade sangria with a vivacious shepherdess, only to be interrupted by her husband, who was thought to be at the fishmonger's. Stefan seemed annoyed with this tale and walked out of the room.

I followed him into the kitchen, where he was slogging down crème de cassis straight from the bottle. I asked him if he was all right.

He wiped his mouth angrily on an antique linen tea towel. "I am sick of that tedious story about the Andalusian shepherdess! It was a long time ago, and it still brings up unpleasant memories."

"I know what you mean," I said. "That's just how I feel whenever Val recounts the 1988 Van Halen concert at Soldier Field when Sammy Hagar fell off the stage and injured himself with a bottle of tequila that had been stuck in his spandex."

Stefan slammed down the liqueur and said, "What the hell does that mean? It's not the same thing at all."

"Yes, it is. It was the same night my grandfather died, May eighth, but Val always forgets that. Grandfather was sick in the hospital for a long time, but we were too busy trolling the country in a minibus to go visit him before he died. Which brings up, as you say, unpleasant memories."

Stefan blinked at me a few times, then handed me the bottle. Then he said, "Sometimes you're all right."

First, party admittance, then grudging regard! The progress I have made with 2F astounds me.

"Let's move it outside!" shouted Chung from the lounge. Somehow I found the Lemming and he handed me a Kir Royale. Unfortunately, I lost him in the throng as the fifty of us trooped down the stairs to the backyard.

Stefan set up a portable stereo on the picnic table and tiki torches on the lawn. Many of our garden flowers had begun to bloom over the last month and made a pretty setting for the party. I sat with Paco in a plastic deck chair at the edge of the patio (the giantess was doing the bus stop by the peonies with the lonely drifter from 1R). The Lemming pushed his way through the crowd and sat with us.

"What a bore," he sighed, lapping pettishly at his Kir Royale.

Val Wayne came over and pulled me up, enticing me to dance with him. He churned his hips around and circled me, Paco clapped his hands in time with the music, and I frugged like there was no tomorrow. The Lemming looked like he was going to be ill.

"You dance like Bruce Springsteen," he said. Hooray! Modern hipness is something that usually evades me.

At the back of the patio, I saw Fat Bald Jeff talking with Francis. Instead of the grandpa sweater and soiled jeans, Francis wore an extremely snug vest and cleanish trousers. His silky shirt gaped open and the flyaway collars draped over his shoulders. A magnetic force drew me in, like the slutty girls who were drawn to Val. I floated over to Francis, staring at the wild chest hair struggling to break free from the confines of buttons and cloth.

I interrupted their conversation, but no amount of etiquette training could have saved me; my reaction was primal and savage. I reached out and touched the tip of the flapping collar.

I rasped, "This is what Yanni wore when he played his concert in the Acropolis and made his mother cry." I may have drooled, but savagery such as mine cannot be controlled where Yanni is concerned.

Francis replied, "Uh . . . yes." He nervously smoothed down his shirt and pushed his black hair out of his face. Jeff rolled his eyes to the heavens.

"Care to dance?" asked Francis.

I removed my spectacles. The previous bout of frugging taught me I am apt to lose my balance midprance, and I did not want to squash them.

"No," he said, putting them back on the bridge of my nose. "Keep them on. They're kind of sexy."

We danced together. Really close. I got a fluttery, anxious feeling in my stomach, just like when I found a real Kate Spade pencil pouch in the dollar bin at the thrift.

After the song, Val walked by and nudged me, whispering, "Nice going! You know what it means when a man can dance well."

Of course I do. It means his parents had the good sense to enroll him in dancing class in junior high, and that he probably has decent manners as well. Score!

Fat Bald Jeff had started to move away from us when he stopped abruptly, inclining his head toward the apartments next door. He strained, listening for something. "There it is again," said Jeff suddenly. "Listen." Down the gangway between my building and the next came a high squealing cry. Jeff told Francis all about the beheading and subsequent nightmares the whining white pup had evoked.

I said, "The fence over there is broken." We all looked at the chain-link fence separating the alley from the back of the neighboring building. Part of it had been pulled away, revealing a means of entrance.

A moment of expectant silence, then Jeff said, "Oh, no."

Francis said, "Right. I'll bring my car around."

Ten minutes later, Francis and I sat waiting in the car two blocks away. We parked on a dark side street underneath a burned-out street lamp.

Why, just three months ago I was boiling up simple beige foods for supper without a thought to my fellow man or beast, and the next thing I knew, I was inciting rebellion in coworkers and participating in an animal liberation plot. Somehow a sullen bloated computer geek had inspired me to revolution—I, formerly one of the hordes of complacent, gullible fools at work, have become somewhat brave, a little daring, and sort of productive. Sure, Jeff may live in a shanty and eat canned goods by the boatload; he may bathe, however infrequently, in a metal apple-bobbing tub; he may slaughter attacking pets; he may have a ribbon of misanthropy running through his soul; but he has a good heart underneath all the flesh, however clogged with cholesterol its arteries may be.

"Here he comes," said Francis, and sure enough, Fat Bald Jeff emerged from the dark alley. One could scarcely notice the extra bulge under his jean jacket, though we saw a small fuzzy white head peek out between the buttons of his coat.

We dropped Jeff and the puppy off at the hovel while we went to the store for dog food and squeaky toys. When we returned, Jeff had fallen asleep on the crusty futon, the pup snoozing peacefully atop his mammoth belly. He stirred in his sleep, opened an eye groggily, and muttered, "I'm calling him Zero."

He claimed it was because he had finally made something out of the "nothing" of his life. But I think it's from the Zero candy bar that started our whole adventure.

Francis and I drove back to the party. Realized I had completely forgotten about the Lemming, leaving him there without any explanation; also realized I didn't care. At the intersection of Damen and Fullerton, a street vendor lurched into traffic, wielding a white bucket, and stumbled from car to car. Francis rolled down his window and motioned to him. He handed the vendor a bill, and the vendor withdrew one of those electric red roses from the bucket.

Driving away, Francis handed me the thing and said, "I wish it were real, but at least this one will last longer."

A tiny tear escaped my eye as I clutched the simulated, neon blossom. Who needs *The Language of Flowers*? Everybody knows what a red rose means.